THE TRIUMPHS OF KAHURU

THE SAGA OF THE HUMAN LEOPARD CONTINUES.

A novel by
Sebati Edward Mafate

"The Triumphs of Kahuru," by Sebati Edward Mafate. ISBN 978-1-949756-21-0 (softcover); 978-1-949756-22-7 (eBook).

Published 2019 by Virtualbookworm.com Publishing Inc., P.O. Box 9949, College Station, TX , 77842, US.

TABLE OF CONTENTS

DEDICATION

For Lucas MaPoulo, father of a great friend whom I have considered a blood brother. And to the great friend, Mpho MaPoulo, for all the years that I have known him and his beautiful family. Also, for my father, Michael "Bra Mike" Mafate, thanks for being a great father till the end.

PROLOGUE

IT WAS STILL IN THE VERY ODD HOURS of the morning, but Henry Thomas Davies paced back and forth in his bedroom. He was not an insomniac, but something about that night kept him awake. This was surprising because he had spent the past three months in a stagecoach, beaten by the harsh outdoors—the aftereffects of a journey that had started in Boston and had ended back home on a plantation in Mississippi; this, after a three-year absence.

Henry, now twenty-four years old, knew right there and then that his life was on the verge of taking a dramatic turn. Perhaps for the better, perhaps for the worst, but for his sake, he hoped for the former. He stretched his arms and walked over to the old clock at the other side of the room. The ground still shook, and his head still whirled from the effects of that long journey. As for his body, that was just one big sore. He looked at the clock and made the necessary mental subtractions. It always kept the wrong time for as long as he could remember. It was a quarter to three in the AM.

The previous night, he had a dream. The dream was familiar even though he could not recall the specifics, but a cold sweat, after he woke up, trickled down his spine asking him the same questions he had always asked himself. "Did the human leopard known as Kahuru really exist? Was there such a thing as a magic spear, otherwise known as the spear of Good? Was there a nation at the southern part of the "Dark Continent" known as the Bakhudung? Where according to lore (which Melvin and others swore was fact) the great Kahuru originate?"

This fascination had become a lifelong obsession. The fact was that Melvin Davies, the slave from Africa, had told him when they were both much younger, and many years thereafter, that he had seen the human leopard. He always put it as: "*with these two very eyes Henry*".

Henry paced around the room and looked through the window from which he always sneaked out for many years to the slave cabins down below. It was this window that had kept a forbidden friendship as alive as a roaring flame. The plantation was quiet because it was devoid of life. Although this was the height of summer, a cool, early morning breeze from the east came through the window.

He thought of Melvin (whose real name was Sanza Kazadi) and fought back tears. Perhaps it was for this exact same reason why he went to Boston, Massachusetts, where he enrolled at Harvard University and received degrees in Archeology and Linguistics. Perhaps that is why he had decided to set up an expedition to Africa and find Kahuru - not only to seek a name for himself, but maybe that would be the time when his mind would finally be at ease.

It was the time for a lifelong desire and quest to be fulfilled, and this is one of the most popular versions of this story.

PART 1

CHAPTER 1

THE FIRST STREAKS OF LIGHT from the eastern horizon announced daybreak. It was time for the worshippers to return to the village. The river god, Nzuzi, had acknowledged their thanks. Landu and Mpiko Kazadi were now officially proud parents of a bouncing baby boy they had named Sanza.

There was joy and jubilation as the couple and three friends, including a renowned medicine man, headed back to the village along a narrow meandering path. In the past, Landu Kazadi had offered numerous sacrifices in an all-out attempt to invoke the river god - for it was believed that it was only through him that children were brought to this World. As an ivory dealer, (he hunted elephants and sold its tusks to the Arabs) Landu prayed for nothing but sons, sons who would take over the trade after he left this earth as his father had done. This was a custom passed from father to son.

However, his wife, Mpiko Kazadi, then the most desirable woman among all the villages along the great Kongo River, bore him four girls in rapid succession, a fact that had troubled Landu deeply. It was for this reason why the hunter thought of taking another wife, but before making that decision, he gave it one more try, this time with the help of the village medicine man. He began offering sacrifices to the river god, which among other things, included the tip of his little finger.

It was early in the morning, but the tropical heat and humidity were beginning to take their toll. He was already breaking into a sweat as he peaked over his wife's shoulder to look at his newborn, who was neatly wrapped in numerous rags. He was a bundle of joy, tiny, helpless, and sound asleep. The quacking of parrots, the chattering of monkeys, and numerous other sounds of this primeval forest were music to his ears.

As they all silently walked towards the village, Landu's mind floated back to that night a season and a half earlier, the night when he decided to make a final appeal to the river god. It had been raining continuously since mid-afternoon that day. He had just finished mending his nets in preparation for the great fishing period, which came at least three times in one season, and was when, for some reason, the Kongo River would run with less ferocity and would beg the villagers to fish from it. This was a phenomenon nobody could explain—there were, of course, too many myths and legends behind it.

Since the weather was not even conducive for hunting, he retired to his hut after the midday meal and had time to ponder. Landu Kazadi was a great ivory hunter and was well known throughout the land stretching into the depths of the forest where the Bambuti lived, a race of pygmies well known for their great hunting prowess. His father was also a hunter; so Landu desperately needed an heir to continue the legacy.

He needed a son, and there was no question about it. The family name was to resound until the end of time, but when he thought of his wife, his heart was filled with despair. Unlike most men in his village, Landu felt he only needed one woman in his life to satisfy him. This was strange, for it was custom for a man to have at least two wives. So, when Mpiko bore him girls, one after the other, he knew he had to succumb to the pressure of finding another bride who would hopefully give him a son, a decision that greatly distressed the hunter for he loved his wife dearly.

It was then that he decided to see Okito-Sodo, the renowned medicine man. After pushing his fishing nets aside and stretching his well-toned limbs, the hunter stepped into the late afternoon rain and strode towards the medicine man's compound. The Azizi village was comprised of no more than fifty families at the time. Moments later, the hunter was standing in front of the medicine man's door, clearing his throat and still unsure if this was a wise decision.

"Why don't you come in, Landu? The weather is bad, as you can see," a voice from the hut sounded. The hunter was startled but quickly composed himself.

It was dark in the hut. A small fire at the center of the room gave little light, which reduced the medicine man's figure to a silhouette. He was facing the eastern side of the hut, which meant his back was turned to the entrance.

"Sit down." It was a command.

Landu complied as he looked around the hut. His eyes were already accustomed to the semi-darkness. There were all sorts of beads, cowries, and animal tails hanging from the sides of the hut. To his right, there were two stools surrounded by earthenware pots. One was filled with water and the other with skulls, animal skulls, although he thought one of them looked human. The last observation sent a cold chill down his spine.

"You came to see me about having a baby boy, correct?"

Landu was already used to the medicine man's proverbial accuracy and was always impressed each time.

"Yes, O great one. It is such as you speak."

"Good, so that means you already know what has to be done."

Landu ought to have sacrificed a white cock in the privacy of his hut the night before.

"Yes, O great one. The sacrifice was done."

"And that's why you are here."

"That is why I am here, O great one," Landu concurred.

"Good. Now, this is what I want you to do." Okido-Sado went on to describe in great detail what was needed and what was to be done. In short, the hunter was to go back to his hut and stay in there without any disturbance. During this time, he would be applying a special ointment to his little finger. This ointment had a soothing and anesthetic effect. It was made from special leaves and roots known only to a few medicine men.

Then after the first crow, which came shortly after midnight, the hunter was to be naked, except for a strip of loincloth. Using the family machete (every family had one), he was to cut off clean the tip of his finger. The hunter was not to scream, for it was believed that if he did, he would have cursed his son to a life of cowardice and fear.

The first crow found Landu standing in the middle of his hut, his machete raised and his left palm resting on a log. The little finger was spaced as far away from the rest as possible. He grinded his teeth as he folded the other four fingers, starting with his thumb. His brow was dark with perspiration. The rain had long ceased, and as a result, there were many night sounds of the tropical forest that filled the night.

He closed his eyes but immediately opened them when he remembered the medicine man's stern warning. He was to keep them open all throughout the ordeal. This meant that his unborn son would never fear the unknown. Bravery was a priceless virtue every father wished upon his son. So, what was cutting off the tip of his finger without a scream?

With no further hesitation, Landu sliced off the tip of his finger. He had never experienced such excruciating a pain in his entire life. It was only miraculous that he did not cry out. Instead, tears flowed freely along his cheeks as he swallowed hot saliva. After tucking the white cock, he had beheaded under his left armpit, he ran mightily towards Okito-Sodo's hut, leaving a small trail of blood behind him.

Upon reaching the medicine man's hut, the latter was chanting incantations in a voice hardly recognizable as his. Without a word, he signaled the hunter to follow him. They ran along the main path leading to the great river. The forest thickened until the path became a tunnel in the woods. The soil changed from loose, dark loam to slippery, white clay. Meanwhile, Landu's hand was on fire. By the time they reached the river, his maimed finger was swollen as though filled with air.

Following more incantations, the cock and the piece of his finger were tossed into the flowing water. As they turned to retrace their footsteps, thunder cracked followed by lightning. In that brief moment of light, Landu thought he saw several human-like figures emerge from the water and race towards them. They were spirits, both good and evil. He was to show no fear even though all that was happening was tough to behold.

He was even instructed not to, even for a slight moment, glance over his shoulder or to the sides as the two of them raced back to the village. By this time, the footsteps behind them were getting ever closer no matter how fast they ran. It was only after the first hut was in sight that the sounds behind them stopped as suddenly as they had begun. Nonetheless, the two men did not stop running until they were in the safety of the medicine man's hut.

During the pursuit, Landu had forgotten all about his throbbing wound. As soon as the two men caught their breath, Okito-Sodo pulled out his famous medicine bag and began treating the wound. It was after this that the medicine man finally spoke up:

"You did well, son of Kazadi. The river god, Nzuzi, has granted your wish. You will have a son named Sanza Kazadi."

And that was how it came to pass. As they silently walked the same path, he and the medicine man took that night, which now seemed like ages before, Landu could not help but smile as he once more glanced at the little finger or rather, what was left of it. He saw life with true meaning. There was at last an heir who was to continue the Kazadi legacy—a legacy of great hunters and braves.

With this thought in mind, Landu vowed to protect his son with his life. He had even offered countless sacrifices to the gods and family ancestors. These sacrifices were essential for the wellbeing of his newborn until he was old enough to take care of himself because these were dangerous times. Children disappeared all the time, not only from his village but also from many others, far and wide. It was strongly believed, and rightly so, that they were snatched and sold into slavery.

Upon arriving at the village, the worshippers were met by an entire village that was ready to celebrate the arrival of its brand-new member. As such merrymaking took its course and a feast was arranged, which went on days on end, Landu Kazadi's mind and spirit were now at ease. His wife could bear as many girls as she wished. He now had a boy who he would address as "my son" for the rest of his days.

CHAPTER 2

THE BOY, SANZA, BLOSSOMED like a mushroom as seasons flew by like doves. By the time he was eight seasons old, he was quite a bit taller and bigger than his playmates. He possessed qualities that were rare among children who came from families of all girls.

The young Sanza was not pampered like one might expect. On the contrary his father would always push him into danger such as taking him on hunting expeditions as soon as he turned six. Landu taught him how to set traps for small animals like hare, rock rabbits, and even antelopes. By his seventh birthday, Sanza could imitate sounds of the rarest tropical night birds. He could name and identify plants, roots, and even leaves, which only a handful of adolescents could name.

Landu, being a part time farmer, also encouraged his son to tread along with him to far off fields. Mpiko, his wife, complained often bitterly to her husband that he was being too hard on the boy even though he had not grown hair around his pubic area. The hunter would counter by saying that his wife was trying to turn their son into a woman, who would be of no use to their village or even to carry on their great family legacy.

Mpiko would continue by accusing her husband of not letting the young Sanza be a child like all others. But then, the hunter would point at the stub on his left hand. That pain was what he had to go through for them to have a son. He would then go on and relate the events of that dreadful night, each time adding embellishments that were not quite related to what actually happened, but nonetheless, made the episode scarier than it really was. Having heard this song many times over, Mpiko would shut up. Besides, it was unheard of for a woman to argue back and forth with her husband.

In any case, as the young Sanza began to understand his surroundings and the village, his father would lecture him every night in his hut. They were living in dangerous times, Landu would say. People, including children, disappeared without a trace and were never heard of again. These disappearances happened all the time. It was said that they were sold into slavery. Sanza was not to trust anybody, except of course, members of his immediate family.

He was not to enter people's houses without his father's prior consent. It was known that certain villagers collaborated with the slave dealers for a price. For these kinds of people, children were an easy target. There was a story of Diomi, who was once found with priceless items in his possession. When pressured into saying where he got these items from and after gruesome sessions of torture, Diomi confessed to being an associate with the Arabs, well known slave dealers.

Above all Sanza, was warned to always run away whenever he saw these men; they were dangerous and not to be trifled with.

"But father," the young Sanza asked one day. "You deal with the Arabs all the time. Why do you say they are dangerous people?"

Landu stroked his chin for a while before answering his son.

"Sanza, one thing you must understand is that your father is a great ivory hunter like your grandfather was. The Arabs love ivory, and the only way they can get it is through me, so that's why they cannot lay a finger on me. Besides, during my meetings with them, I come well-armed and accompanied by warriors from our village. Although I do not expect any trouble from them, it is always wise to allow for danger even when there is none."

Father and son sat in silence for a while before Sanza said, "But father, when you hunt, you hunt alone. Are you not afraid of getting taken?"

He had been warned time and again never to wander off in the forest by himself. There lay unspeakable dangers, which included being kidnapped by slave hunters.

"Ha-ha, you see this?" Landu pointed at an amulet dangling from a string around his neck. "This, my son, makes me quick, nimble, and invisible when I am alone in the forest. It was made by some famous medicine man who lived among the Bambuti. It was made for your great grandfather, who in turn, passed it to my father then to me. In time, it will be yours, and you will pass it on to your sons. This amulet, Sanza, is what keeps me safe."

He went on to relate the family history dating back to the 1400's. He spoke of the great wars with other villages and the roles his forefathers played in the formation of their village and clan—The Azizi. While hearing the stories, young Sanza's mind would float to places unheard of. He could hear the battle cries, the cries of fear, death, and mayhem as his ancestors brought about order in a land once governed by chaos. It is safe to say the little boy was destined for greatness like his father and a long string of fathers before him.

Unlike most children, nightfall would find Sanza in his father's hut, where he would sit at his feet and listen to tales of the night and terror. At this time, children his age would be listening to their mothers' folktales or watching them prepare the evening meals for their husbands. This was the norm, and everybody agreed that Sanza was an unusual child, most probably a reincarnation of his grandfather.

Little did anybody know that tragedy was knocking at the door. The young Sanza was being targeted. There was a pair of eyes that studied the movements of this child with the zeal of a high priest of the river god. These eyes took the shape of a man in his early thirties, a fellow villager and a young man by the name of Masamba Kali.

CHAPTER 3

AT THIRTY-THREE SEASONS, Masamba Kali was by no means a very successful man. His parents had died when he was about twelve, and he had since been raised by his uncle who lived at a neighboring village less than half days walk away. The fact that his parents had died at a rather early age meant that he had no inheritance he could call his own. The little that his parents owned was quickly grabbed and divided amongst greedy relatives masquerading as people looking out for the wellbeing of the young orphan. As a result, the young Masamba had to work his nails off in his uncles' fields, which produced less and less as seasons went by.

Masamba had a bitter issue against the Azizi village. This bitterness was because his uncle, Wazola, had hammered into his young mind that his parent's death was not due to natural causes. He insisted that they were in fact, poisoned. The truth of the matter is that nobody knew what the real causes of his or her deaths were. There were many stories, and it is now difficult to tell which one is true.

However, the story that Mbanza Kali once came from the heart of the forest with some rare looking mushrooms, which he asked his wife to cook, is well authenticated. That the young Masamba did not eat from this pot, as he was visiting relatives, strengthens the belief that the mushrooms Mbanza picked from the forest that fateful day had a lot to do with their untimely death.

Nonetheless, Wazola overlooked this fact and insisted that the whole story was a cover up. Masamba's parents were murdered, plain and simple. Why, because the couple was destined for wealth and prosperity. This was Wazola's version, and it served its intended purpose because Masamba Kali grew up to be a very bitter man.

As expected, he hated everything to do with the village, especially if it was something good. For instance, a village hunt called for a degree of intimacy among the villagers, meaning that every man was required to partake in the hunting of animals, whose carcasses were to be shared among all members of the village. Masamba often grumbled when asked or rather, told to partake in the hunt of a certain animal—told because refusal was unheard of.

Even after the hunt, Masamba would not be satisfied with his share, and he would growl and complain until he got even more than the most able hunter who, in most instances, received a fraction of what he deserved. Many villagers interpreted this kind of behavior as a cry for help from a child who knew not the warmth of a mother's love.

Nobody had any idea that it was his uncle from the Baluba village who was behind it. Yes, it was Wazola who convinced Masamba to marry from his (Wazola's) village. His word was the only kind of law Masamba could obey. Thus, it was easy to initiate his nephew into the lucrative trade of slavery with the Arabs, who crossed the great waters of the east into their lands.

So, when Wazola asked his nephew if there was a viable prospect the young man could kidnap from his village with the help of one of his most trusted right hand man, Masamba did not hesitate. The promise of untold riches helped a lot in influencing his decision. The victim had to be young—very young and strong—one who could endure immense hardship only known to slavery. This prospect would hike a good price from the Arab slave dealers.

Masamba knew who the intended victim would have to be without giving it too much thought: Sanza the only son of Landu and Mpiko Kazadi. The boy would have to be kidnapped before the next full moon, which was about eight days away. This required care and meticulous planning from Masamba and his partner-in-crime, a young man named Fulani sent by his uncle, because they would have to steal the child from under his parents' noses.

The job was bound to be easy because Fulani had led many exploits like this one. Thus, the two young men waited patiently for the opportunity to present itself. Their plan was going to succeed. Failure was not an option or else they were dead meat.

———

It had been a long day for Landu Kazadi, perhaps a day he would live never to forget. He had woken up very early that morning, and after selecting the weapons he needed, he set off. It had been reported that a herd of elephants had been roaming not too far from the village. Since this was not too far a distance to travel, he decided to bring his son along. Now almost thirteen seasons old, the hunter felt this was the right time for his son to start learning the trade.

On the other hand, Sanza could not contain his excitement. He could hardly sleep after his father unexpectedly came over to him and announced that the time had finally come for him to go on a real hunting trip. Hence, it was little wonder that when Landu came to wake him up, he found his only son up and ready to go, already dressed in the mini hunting regalia his mother had made for him. Strapped to his waist was a machete a little too big and heavy for him, but which,nonetheless, made him feel like a real hunter, if not a seasoned warrior.

They left before dawn, without a word to anybody. It was still dark, and the morning star was just getting ready to set. Father and son walked through the forest, taking numerous paths that looked like dark tunnels. Before long, the village was left far behind. Landu maintained a steady pace that seemed difficult for Sanza, as he, on numerous occasions, had to trot in order to catch up with his father.

The thick forest was alive with noises coming from different animals, especially from the colobus monkeys that chattered from overhead branches, which intertwined and formed a roof. It was already sunrise when the two broke out of the forest and came to an open veld after crossing one of the numerous streams that poured into the great river.

Landu Kazadi immediately stopped and bent on one knee. His son followed suit. For a long time, he gazed at the distance ahead. Without a word, he signaled his son to crawl forward towards him. Apparently, they were getting closer to the herd they were looking for because Sanza realized, for the first time, some fresh elephant dung amidst the long grass that was still wet with dew.

His father cleared his throat noiselessly and said, "Son, we are not too far from the herd. Remember, we are only after one particular bull, the oldest."

It was the first time he had uttered a word ever since they left the village. Next, he laid down the quiver filled with arrows that had been slinging from his shoulder. These particular arrows were quite long, a little longer than a man's arm and were special arrows, for they were made out of iron. Their razor thin sharpness gave them an almost accurate aim. Sanza thought, and rightly so, that they must have cost his father a fortune for they had to have been specially made by a renown black smith who lived as a hermit in a land far off.

"Qualities of a good hunter are, among other things, making sure that his quiver is always full and knowing what kind of animals to strike at first. For instance, you must never under any circumstances, if you can help it, kill an animal that is heavy with child or if it's young, still depends on its mother for its survival."

Landu had already tested his enormous bow several times and as an added precaution, tied another elastic string to it for maximum power. His hands worked with the regularity and efficiency of a machine. In his young mind, Sanza wondered if he would ever become that good.

"And remember, son," Landu continued as he stretched his bow and fitted an arrow into it before making a mock aim at the sky, "Patience is the hunter and warrior's most important virtue."

He then took the long goatskin bag that he had asked his son to carry. The weight had been tiresome, but he dared not open his mouth for his father would have considered him equal to his sisters and not worthy of being called a hunter. The bag contained a long stick with a hole in it. Sanza knew it only as the "thunder stick," for he was told that it spat smoke and fire before producing a deafening noise. Above all, it could drop anything dead from a long distance. This, of course, was Landu Kazadi's most prized possession. He had bought it from the Arabs many seasons earlier.

Sanza watched his father break the stick in half before stuffing some strange looking powder into it, thereafter, putting it back together, again. It was common knowledge that only his father owned this magic stick.

When all was ready, the hunter stood up, swung his bow and arrows over his right shoulder, and held the stick in his left hand. Sanza looked at him questioningly, and the hunter read his mind.

"One can never rely solely on one weapon, especially on a hunt of this magnitude," he said.

They began walking, again. This time, Sanza did not trot behind but instead, walked side by side with this famous hunter. His heart fluttered and raced with intense excitement. Beside it was another heart over a quarter and a half century older, beating with little or no excitement, persuading older blood to flow through arteries not any less old.

They arrived at last at the escarpment, where they gazed at the magnificent elephant herd, below. There were over fifteen of them grazing with their calves. The female cows surpassed the males in number, to which, Landu pointed out that their way of life was similar to that of humans. The beasts observed very strong family ties, and the herd they were looking at was in fact, a tribe.

Among the herd was the largest, with equally large ears that flapped benevolently back and forth. It had long and prominent tasks, twice as long as the rest. This was no doubt the leader of the clan and also, the oldest. It immediately occurred to Sanza that as far as his father was concerned, this was the one that had to go. The beast was as magnificent and majestic as the great continent of Africa.

They sat at the escarpment and waited. By mid-morning, the fierce rays of the tropical sun began to pierce down at them. There was no ceiling of leaves and branches to protect them from the already scorching heat, but Landu did not move an inch. Instead, he ordered his son to bring out the food they had carried along. Sanza opened two parcels of coco, yam and plantain leaves, revealing yams boiled in blood red oil. They ate in silence. All this time, Landu had not taken his gaze away from the sight, below. On the other hand, Sanza was wondering what they were waiting for.

Towards noon, he got his answer. The ancient beast slowly walked away from the rest of its herd, a move that was not lost to the hunter, for he quickly said to his son after inspecting his weapons one last time:

"Quickly son, now is the time." He was already heading downhill before his son would ask any questions.

Once in the little valley, they lost sight of the elephant because of the long grass. This proved to be short-lived, because after a while, the landscape broke open into a little veld, and right in front of them, was the lone bull still walking northwards away from his clan.

Landu quickly whispered instructions to his son, whose heartbeat sped to an alarming rate, threatening to burst open his little rib cage. The plan was simple and yet, effective. Sanza was to run as fast as he could and stand directly in front of the elephant's path—at a very safe distance, of course.

The beast was going to stop and size him up for a moment. This would give Landu ample time to attack from the side, delivering a blow that was to incapacitate the elephant. It was believed that an elephant's weakest spot was on the side, somewhere between the head and the neck. Landu had warned his son that this would be a tough sight to behold and that what he was seeing was even larger than the biggest hut in the village. Above all, it would be a test for Sanza—a test of courage and manhood and a test to see if he had what it took to be a great hunter like his father or grandfather. It was a test at which he could not fail.

If, however, the elephant decided to charge, he was to turn around and run in a zigzag fashion. Running straight would be suicidal. Sanza did as he was told. The sight of the enormous elephant was breathtaking, more frightening than his father had led him to believe.

The elephant paused and looked at the diminutive figure ahead of him. He raised his trunk and let out an earsplitting roar. Sanza's knees wobbled as he thought of his oncoming doom. Urine flowed freely on his leg as terror released his bladder.

For a moment, nothing happened. The elephant kept looking at him as it grazed its front foot on the soft ground. The great beast raised his trunk and trumpeted again, then charged. The ground shook as the elephant made for Sanza, who was rooted at one spot—paralyzed in mind and body with fear.

The beast was fairly close when Landu shouted, "Run, Sanza... run!" There was unmistakable panic in his voice.

The bull elephant was almost within striking distance when Sanza finally took to his heels. He ran with all the energy that the fear of death could conjure. However, Sanza had forgotten the most crucial warning, to run in a zigzag manner. Although he dodged trees and undergrowth with uncanny dexterity, the elephant quickly cut the distance between them.

On seeing the quickly diminishing distance between the elephant and his fleeing son, Landu took an aim with his bow and arrow. The elephant was just about to stretch its trunk and grab Sanza when the arrow struck. It was not a deathblow but nonetheless, made the beast pause in his mad charge. The arrow was sticking from his side as he now turned to face his assailant.

With steady hands, Landu lifted the magic stick and fired. The noise was so loud that hundreds of birds from surrounding trees took fright and fled, but the magnificent animal did not fall. Instead, his pace was now reduced to an unsteady walk. Landu stuffed more powder into the stick and fired, again. This time, the elephant succumbed as his forehead was split open by the impact of the bullet.

For a long time, Landu Kazadi looked at the fallen animal as a few reflex actions twitched its trunk. He was sweating profusely as he tried to calm his shaking body. For the first time, he felt fear, the kind of fear a father experiences when he almost witnessed first-hand the death of his only son. Landu blamed himself for pushing his son into grave danger at such an early age.

Mpiko was right. He was trying too hard to make a man out of a boy who had barely reached his thirteenth birthday. He called out to his son, but there was no response. He then went looking for him until he found him hiding in a long-deserted anteater's hole.

He looked at the panic-stricken child for a moment, fighting back stinging tears, before stretching out his hand.

"Come, my son. You did well. I am proud of you; so are your ancestors."

To Sanza, no other words could have sounded sweeter. He had thought that respect from his father was now a fantasy. Thus, it was with pride that he helped his father de-tusk the elephant, thinking not for one moment about how close he had been to death. It was late in the afternoon when father and son headed back to the village, each carrying the ultimate trophy on his shoulder. As for the carcass, all that the villagers had to see were the tusks, and endless trips with baskets to the kill would follow, that is, if the Hyenas and other scavengers did not beat them to it.

That evening, Landu and his son went to bed early. Normally, Landu would let his son doze at his feet, but for some reason, Landu insisted on his son sleeping in his own little hut for the first time. Sanza lay on his little bamboo bed, replaying that day's adventure in his mind, and before long, he was sound asleep.

Presently, he found himself awake. He did not know why he woke so suddenly, but he had a feeling that a noise had roused him. Then Landu's dog began to bark, but that was its habit. It had probably seen a jackal or something. Again, the boy fell into a light sleep.

Soon, a loud bang woke him up, and he sat upright on his bed to face a wide gap where the door had once been. The next moment, two figures entered the room, and before he could shout, a rag was stuffed into his mouth almost instantaneously and his hands held behind him as he was blindfolded. The men carried him outside and away, making as little noise as possible. When they reached the main village path, they sat him down, took off his blind, and ordered him to walk along. He tried to struggle the entire time, thinking that he was in a grip of a terribly vivid nightmare, but a smack on his buttocks convinced him that the men were not to be trifled with. What was worse was that he could not cry out. He walked along with the men until they passed the outskirts of the village. Then, he saw two other boys (in similar conditions, though) tied to a tree. The two men untied them from the tree and joined Sanza and soon, the village was left far behind.

"Good work, Fulani," Masamba said as he patted his colleague's back.

"Ummmm," Fulani grunted his approval.

That morning, Landu woke up only to be confronted by the gaping entrance of what had once been his son's door, and right there and then, the hunter knew that the son he cherished more than anything else in this world was gone, lost to him and the village forever. He cursed the day he had gone to see Okito-Sodo, the renowned medicine man, in his all-out quest for a son.

CHAPTER 4

WHEN SANZA CAME TO, he could hardly breathe from shock and terror. His hands were cut and bruised from the long night's walk. He had heard of people being abducted from the village, never to be heard of again. He never imagined this could ever happen to him, despite the numerous warnings from his parents and close relatives, he never imagined that this would happen to him.It was still a nightmare to him when he recalled the dark figures that broke into his hut without warning, a nightmare he would soon awake from. But when he felt the numerous prodding with sharp sticks on his back and the whippings urging him to keep walking, Sanza Kazadi knew this was no dream. He was never going to see his family again. The feeling was overwhelming, beyond shock and grief.

Upon entering the great forest, they were blindfolded, again, shackled, and yoked in one long line. The blindfolds were removed after they walked all night. It was close to dawn when they were ordered to stop and camp. It took a while for Sanza to re-orientate himself with his surroundings. They were entirely in very unfamiliar territory. He soon realized they were in more of a similar state, mostly men, a few women, and eight children his age. Five were his playmates. The only signs of recognition they had of each other were the downcast faces that reflected fear of the unknown. To Sanza, they all looked like strangers just about to be offered as sacrificial lambs.

Close to mid-day, they were fed with heavily rationed food and water. It was only then that Sanza had a closer look at their captors and instantly recognized Masamba Kali, talking loudly, freely, and happily. Sanza had heard from fellow villagers that Masamba was arrogant and self-seeking, but the boy never expected treachery to this scale. In his young mind, Sanza cursed Masamba and prayed to the gods of retribution to do justice.

As Sanza looked at the traitor, his heart was filled with hatred, which was unavoidable. The type of bravado only common to men at bay replaced this. He balled his tiny fists and clenched his jaws. The next reaction even startled him.

"*Moteki*! Traitor!"

Sanza's shrill voice frightened the overhead gray parrots, which started squawking in unison.

He sprang at Masamba with youthful elasticity. Only the shackles around his neck and arms prevented what according to him, would have been a death charge to rip Masamba's eyeballs off their sockets.

"Shut your mouth... you filthy little monkey!" Masamba spat out and immediately reached for his whip.

It took numerous whippings from him before Sanza was subdued. At last, the lad collapsed, and for the first time since his capture, he wept for a long time before falling into a deep sleep. The women shed tears in sympathy. The rest could only watch and grind their teeth in anger.

Later that evening, the party arrived at a camp with more captives from other villages. They were also under the supervision of black slatees. This was the rendezvous spot because the two Arabs, Suleiman and Tipu-Tik, were present. They were the most notorious of all the slave dealers. Even though Sanza was seeing them for the first time, they were not as scary as they had been in his dreams.

At this camp, all the captives were ordered to carry an elephant task on their shoulder, regardless of age. They were then forced to walk with whips showering on them at regular intervals. The next few days turned to prove that treatment from the black slatees like Masamba was even worse than that of the Arabs, themselves. Life was a nightmare. The journey itself, to some unknown destination, was torture. They walked for a long time, for days on end, yoked and chained to one another. On this second phase of the journey, Sanza was surprised that Fulani, Masamba's counterpart, conversed fluently with the Arabs in their language, an observation not even lost to the youngest of all the captives.

The weight of the tusks was galling. If anyone dropped it, as it always happened, whips would lash out indiscriminately. Escape was a fantasy. Besides, their captors had made it a point to travel at night during the initial stages of their journey. They took many twists and turns in the dense forest, such that after one moon of traveling, they had no idea as to where they were heading and in which direction they were heading, let alone if they were pointed east or west. This confusion meant that if they did manage to escape, their chances of retracing their footsteps home were close to none. And if one escaped, he would be at the mercy of the forest, which offered all sorts of horrors including wild animals, starvation, and even cannibals.

However, something similar to what the young Sanza prayed to the gods for did occur and was to change the course of his life forever. His prayers were answered in the form of Kahuru, the half-man half-leopard, otherwise known as the human leopard. This was an incident that dogged Sanza for the rest of his life and ended up resounding the name, Kahuru, in a land far away.

Kahuru, the leopard man's, name had spread far and wide. To many who had not seen this remarkable being, he was a phantom. Yet to those who had seen him and had witnessed his might first-hand, he was a phenomenon. And this was to be one of the many triumphs of Kahuru.

The night was like any other. It was almost two moons since Sanza's capture when the captives, the slaveholders, and their black slatees laid camp. As usual, there was a bedlam of cries of fatigue, hunger, and agony from the captives. Sanza had since resigned to his fate, and strange as it may seem, he was actually looking forward to their destination or anything that would end this ordeal.

Each day brought new horrors with it. For instance, one of his playmates, a boy named Nzimbi, had fallen ill from the fever. Because Nzimbi could not walk anymore, Suleiman ordered a pit to be dug. In it, a poisonous snake of the cobra family was tossed after making sure that it was first agitated. Thereafter, the sick child was thrown in.

The others were forced to watch as the serpent struck Nzimbi, time and again, until it ran out of venom. And right before their eyes, the tiny, wriggling body of Nzimbi turned blue before he chewed his tongue in sheer agony, a painful reminder that only the strong and healthy would survive. The sight was so horrendous that even the black slatees, including Masamba, shuddered.

Landu Kazadi had often reminded his son that there were people in this world whose hearts had turned to stone, but what Sanza saw that day was a sight removed from reality. He could not define it as cruelty—it was something way beyond.

There was a man who somehow managed to free himself and escape. Only incapacitating wounds and hunger foiled his attempt. He was easily recaptured moments later and fed alive to the crocodiles the next morning. Those who spoke the same language were not chained together, for the Arabs feared a revolt. Thus, what were left for Sanza were his thoughts and an uncertain future.

So, the moment his body hit the ground, he fell into a deep sleep. This was rare because no matter how tired he was, the luxury of a deep sleep was rare. Suleiman and Tipu-Tik, as usual, laid their skin mats on the ground before lying down with the magic sticks, which Sanza came to know as muskets, tucked right beside them. Only the Arabs and a few slatees, including Masamba and Fulani, carried these deadly weapons.

The slatees had little trouble making a big fire, as firewood was more than abundant. They talked and laughed as they sat around the fire, roasting meat and dry cobs with affected unconcern for the hungry eyes that stared at them.

The night, itself, was a silent one, save for the ambivalent insect world. Once in a while, one of the slatees would walk among the sleeping slaves, or those who pretended to be, to check if they were securely shackled and if their feet were still hobbled with knotted rope. Some of the slatees would kick the captives out of spite.

Close to midnight, Masamba excused himself by saying that his bowels were loose. The others exchanged mischievous glances. They knew that he sometimes made up a story just to hide somewhere and catch up on some sleep. But tonight, was different—he had to go.

He negotiated his way through the primeval forest. The creepers on some of the trees were so thick that they looked like ordinary trees. He always made it a point that the campfire was regularly visible from wherever he was because it took a lot less effort to get lost in a forest like this.

He hid behind a thick trunk, stretched his arms, and was just about to squat, when a twig snapped behind him. He whirled just in time to see a dark figure detach itself from the darkness in a swift motion towards him.

Masamba's upbringing had hardened him for whatever life had in store for him. In other words, he grew up to be a brave man. Few things in this world could frighten him, but at that split moment, nothing prepared him for what he saw—something that looked like a leopard standing on two feet, resembling a human being, too. And before he could scream, the monster struck.

The blow was powerful—breaking his jaw in an instant. His mouth was full of blood, and then he felt the powerful hand-claws, covered with fur, grip his head and twist, snapping his neck like a dry twig. His bowels had since evacuated uncontrollably as terror released his sphincter muscle. The creature let go of his victim, and the body crumpled lifelessly to the ground.

Kahuru!

The fabulous creature, half-man half-leopard, let out a silent growl before darting away from Masamba's body and vanishing into the darkness.

It was after a long time that Fulani, back at the camp, began to sense that something was amiss. Masamba had been gone for quite some time now, and his absence was anything but comfortable. The night forest had way too many dangers lurking within, but he knew that his colleague was very capable of taking care of himself. After all, he could always shout if he needed help.

Nonetheless, he snapped his fingers at two of the other slatees and said, "You two, go and see what Masamba is up to."

The two men never came back.

Sanza woke up and rubbed his eyes. Something had woken him up. He sat up and instinctively looked at the fire where the slatees were seated. He could sense that there was panic and confusion because Fulani and the remaining slatees were arguing heatedly among themselves in harsh whispers—a clear attempt to not wake the Arabs. Sanza, now fully awake, began to wonder what was wrong.

"What do you mean you can't go and look for the rest?" Fulani hissed at one of the slatees.

"No, I can't. Something terrible has happened, and I certainly don't want to end up like them," was the man's explanation.

Sanza could tell the man was frightened beyond words. He now watched the men with some interest and was quick to notice that Masamba Kali was one of the missing men and that their absence was what had thrown these men into a panic.

"Go, I say." Fulani pressed on.

"No, let's wait a little longer; I am sure Masamba got lost, and the others are looking for him." The slatee would not budge.

"Coward!" Fulani spat out.

"Okay, why don't you go, brave one?!" the man retorted. He would not have gone even if it was his own mother missing.

"People don't trifle with me," Fulani said as he took a menacing step towards him, but as he was about to lash out, something froze him dead in his tracks. Sanza felt his scrotum shrink and his hair meet in the middle of his head. He quickly glanced at the two Arabs. They were still fast asleep. The slatees glanced at one another and into the surrounding dark forest. The sound came again, this time much closer and more menacing than before.

It was a snarl.

"Leopard," Fulani hissed as he picked up his musket, which he could use very effectively, as Sanza had long noticed.

The other slatees armed themselves with spears as they quickly spread out and assumed strategic positions around the camp. And just as one of the men was about to say something to Fulani, an oversize leopard leaped from the darkness, its claws extended, and landed on him just in time to rip his neck open and sever numerous veins and arteries before ripping open the top of his head. The dome of the skull came away with the scalp, like the top sheared off a soft-boiled egg, and left the brain exposed.

The giant cat disappeared into the long grass before the men could react. They did react, though, but moments later by firing at the position where the beast was last seen. However, their aim was so panic-stricken and clumsy that they missed altogether.

The noise was enough to wake the Arabs and the rest of the captives, who began pulling this way and that way out of fright.

"Fulani, what is happening?" Suleiman asked, his musket ready; so was Tipu-Tik's.

"A leopard m-master," he said as he ran to inspect his colleague's mutilated body, the same man who had refused to go and look for the missing trio.

He bent down to take a closer look, then turned to face the rest. He was just about to open his mouth and say something when a spear struck him in the upper abdomen. It came with such power that it protruded his body and struck the slatee directly behind him, killing the two men instantly.

Then something beyond amazing happened. The spear disengaged and flew back from where it had come—with the same breath-taking speed and power! Everyone, including the Arabs, screamed in shock, disbelief, and fear. They had heard of flying snakes, talking animals, and the like, but a magic spear?

The Arabs fired indiscriminately into the darkness; the slatees threw their spears. Some wondered if running away was a better idea. The pandemonium continued until they all ran out of ammunition. Thereafter, it was all quiet—only the deep breathing of the men was audible, and it was at that exact moment, when Kahuru attacked.

What Sanza Kazadi saw was a dark figure leap from the long grass and land on one of the slatees. He had enough time to break his neck and hurl his spear at a retreating figure. The spear flew back into the owner's paw-hand.

At that moment, Tipu-Tik, like the rest, was thrown into complete panic.

"Suleiman…Suleiman!" he screamed time and again. "What in Allah's name is happening?"

Tipu-Tik was horrified by what he saw. The same could be said about the rest. There was complete calamity at the camp. What they saw was indeed, a strange sight that defied imagination—a man who looked like a leopard and who had a magic spear. He had dark fur on his massive arms and thick-knotted biceps. He had triangular ears, and his face resembled that of a leopard. He had canines and carnassials—these they could see when he hissed like the leopard that he was. The hands were, in fact, paws that maintained their human mechanism. He was dressed in full war regalia, and he had a tail.

Kahuru continued with his onslaught. Two of the slatees were foolish enough to dare his attack, but a single blow from the leopard man's fist knocked them out cold, not to mention that their jaws were broken by the impact. Tipu-Tik was struck on the neck by the magic spear and died instantly. The last of the slatees fell on his knees, calling on the gods to save him.

As for Suleiman, he started retreating backwards into the long grass when the leopard man began approaching him. His knees wobbled as he raised his musket above his head like a club. Then, a sickening sound of sharp metal slicing through flesh and bone was heard. Suleiman's head fell off his shoulders. The trunk withstood the assault for a very brief moment before crumbling to the ground.

Behind Suleiman's decapitated body, a man stood. He was tall and very dark skinned with fierce eyes. His neck was baffled with rings, and the captives immediately recognized him as a member of the Bamongo tribe, a nation known for its brave warriors. He was brandishing a blood-stained machete that had seen many wars. The man was obviously on the leopard man's side.

He walked over to the chained captives, most of whom were still screaming at the top of their voices, pulling this way and that way. It took a lot of effort from the man to calm them down. He spoke their language but in a different dialect— confirming that he was indeed from the Bamongo people. The man assured them that the leopard man meant them no harm. He, in fact, had rescued them from their captors.

"My name is Gatumbo," he said. "And that man is Kahuru, the master of all men and beasts. He conquers evil and brings about peace and goodwill."

There was silence as the now former captives looked at the phenomenon in awe. So, this was Kahuru, the master of men and beast, well known for his great deeds in the land and beyond. Sanza had very vaguely heard about the legend of Kahuru from his father. He could not recall the exact details of the conversation, but he remembered Landu speaking with great admiration about this immortal.

They were unshackled, thereafter, and the remaining slatee, who was still on his knees the entire time, was beaten to a pulp. Neither Kahuru nor Gatumbo stopped the stronger slaves when they broke his arms and legs. This they did this to deliberately prolong the process of his death.

When everyone was calm, they described their ordeal—how they had been kidnapped and handed over to the Arabs to be sold as slaves. Even the young Sanza had to give his own testimony before Kahuru. Though the sight of Kahuru was fearsome (if not ferocious), he felt more safe and secure in his presence than he had ever before.

Kahuru was silent (for the most part) as he sat on a rock a little further away. His eyes glowed in the darkness, and when he spoke, his voice was so terrifying that Sanza thought even the bravest of men would shudder. Only Gatumbo seemed immune to this fear the human leopard wrought.

Escorting the captives to their respective villages was out of question. The Bamongo people had summoned Kahuru from a far-off land. The human leopard, they later found out, was on an assignment to quell a marauding gorilla that had been terrorizing the Bamongo for quite some time.

Therefore, it was agreed that the freed slaves would accompany Kahuru and his party to the Bamongo village, where they would be given shelter and nursed back to strength, then helped to retrace their journey back to their respective villages.

The rest of Kahuru's party, as Sanza and the rest were to find out, were a young[*] lady, who happened to be Kahuru's companion (this woman was more beautiful than a vision), and a young man known as Iyombe, also from Gatumbo's tribe The young woman, Lindiwe, was believed to have come from a nation at the foothills of the great Drakensberg Mountains—a terrestrial known as a land of plenty and never-ending jubilation, a land of the Bakhudung people of the Khudu, and a land where Kahuru, the leopard man, was first seen.

---

[*] See "*Kahuru: The Making of an African Legend.*"

CHAPTER 5

ACCORDING TO LANDU KAZADI (when he first told his son about Kahuru on one of their numerous hunting trips), he had heard about this phenomenon from a chronicler at a village, two days walk away south of their village, on one of his many quests for elephant tusks. Kahuru's legend had spread. It was said he was a warrior sent from the gods, and, thus, possessed superhuman strength and was backed by forces beyond imagination.

Many believed that Kahuru was a phantom, a figment of some dreamer's imagination. There was no possible way in which someone could look like a man and a leopard at the same time. A man of enormous strength maybe, and perhaps behaved like a leopard, but look like one? Impossible. It sounded more like a tale mothers told to their children around a fire.

However, many stories about this metaphysical being started reaching far off villages, some as far as six moons walk away—the Azizi clan being one of them. There were tales of how Kahuru once defeated an army of over fifty, armed only with his brute strength and the ultimate weapon known as the Spear of Good. For the most part, none of these stories were well authenticated, but they did provide a worthwhile bedtime story.

It is difficult, now, to say whether or not Landu believed in the existence of Kahuru. But it is safe to note that the hunter's son was fascinated beyond words, especially when he was younger. He would sometimes see him in his dreams. Though, surprisingly enough, a few seasons later when he was kidnapped, Kahuru was but a distant memory.

Upon reaching the Bamongo village, the freed captives were assigned to their various huts that the village had provided. This had been one of the leopard man's special requests, which he had addressed to the king of the Bamongo, king Mushamuka. It was later on when decided by the king that the freed captives would be returned to their respective villages.

When he heard the news, Sanza was beyond himself with excitement, but alas, nobody among the Bamongo was familiar with the route to his village, so he had to be adopted by one of the families. He warmed up to this idea with time, after realizing that this was a far better alternative to slavery. And who knew, maybe one day he would be able to find his way back home.

Seasons flew by. With time, his village, his people, and even his family became a distant memory. By the time he was sixteen, he was strong, well-built, and by no means a coward. His shooting was good, and he wielded his machete with more dexterity than the average person.

A budding wrestling champion, he was popular among women; adding to that, he had blossomed into a good-looking, young man. By this time, he had maintained two seasons of unbroken victories in the arena. He had to do five more seasons without being beaten; then, he would be champion. And so far, Sanza Kazadi was on the right track.

Life among the Bamongo was peaceful and pleasant. He worked so hard in the fields that even his foster parents became proud of him and treated Sanza as they would their own children. Although he did not turn out to be a great hunter as his father had been, he was a fine warrior for his age. For a long time, it seemed as if the gods had smiled on this lad once more.

Then the blow struck, again. The Bamongo were invaded by a strong nation from the northwestern part of the continent. Following a fierce war that lasted several moons, the Bamongo were heavily defeated. The casualties were breathtaking, and their village was burned to the ground. Upon declaring unconditional surrender, many of the village's surviving youth and maidens were taken as slaves; Sanza Kazadi was among them. They were taken to the present-day Ivory Coast where they were sold off to the white men awaiting in great canoes, to take them across the great waters into the new world—the Americas.

CHAPTER 6

THE AMERICAS

THE SLAVE SHIP FROM AFRICA docked at the harbor of Massachusetts in the spring of 1778. Sanza and four hundred other slaves were dragged to the auction block three days later and sold off to various slave owners (mostly from the south) who owned numerous cotton plantations.

A rich plantation owner named Lloyd Davies bought Sanza and fifty others. He owned several plantations, but the one that was well-known was in Raymond, Mississippi. Lloyd was born from second-generation settlers who had fled religious persecution from England.

Farming ran in the blood of the Davies clan. Thus, upon reaching the new world, they tilled the land with such pure impunity that before long, they became the chief suppliers of tobacco, wheat, and barley in all of New England. They moved to Mississippi after accumulating tons of wealth, although, some say they felt the English colonialists wanted to tax them out of existence.

It did not take them long to really establish themselves in the south. Consequently, the Davies' quickly became the number one supplier of cotton, and it was said that standing in the middle of their plantation, one would never see the beginning or end of their property.

The secret of their success and a system they implemented in their heirs was simple: live by example. In other words, show your subjects that you are no stranger to hard work; treat them well, and they will break their backs for you. Don't give them too much, either; give them enough to keep them working and satisfied.

Thus, the Davies families were known as easy slave owners, and a slave was considered lucky if he was owned by them. Even the slave overseers were handpicked. Unnecessary cruelty was not tolerated, but this did not mean that life on that plantation was paradise.

The Davies were also staunch Christians, so it was no surprise that Sundays were set aside as days of worship. Lloyd Davies conducted the sermons, himself, in the large plantation barn, teaching the slaves, whom he considered heathens, about the word of God and God's son, Jesus Christ. He strongly believed that God created the darker races to be servers of the white men, and he managed to instill the fear of God into their hearts.

The journey to Mississippi was still on another ship, which set sail along the coast and docked at Georgia. Here, Sanza and the rest were transported across the state in numerous horse drawn wagons and reached their final destination in the summer of 1778.

Sanza Kazadi had no idea where he was or what was happening to him. But one brutal and cold fact that he grasped was that he would never see his motherland again. With this thought in mind, and the fact that he had resigned to his fate, he adapted to his new surroundings and life on the plantation much quicker than the average slave fresh from the soils of Africa.

Within six moons, he could speak and understand the master's language. This impressed Lloyd Davies so much that he started offering Sanza, whose name had been changed to Melvin, chores around the main house, which was a sight of wonder. It was said to be the biggest and most beautiful manor in all of Raymond, Mississippi.

His chores included cleaning the kitchen and making sure that the great cooking stove, furnace, and fireplace had a constant supply of firewood. Mrs. Davies also took quite a liking to this hardworking, pleasant, and unassuming lad, who she called "my little nigger."

Being exposed to the house, Sanza met Lloyd Davies' ten-year-old son named Henry Thomas Davies. He was a quiet and reclusive child, but for some unknown reason, he and Sanza clicked. Whenever Sanza was done with his chores, the two would explore the plantation far and wide. Sanza would teach him about the plants, insects, and animals in the forest that surrounded the plantation.

In return, the young Davies would teach Sanza how to read and write. This was done in great secret, of course, because a literate slave was as good as dead. Theirs was a symbiotic relationship, so it was no wonder when one Sunday afternoon Henry, all smiles holding two rabbits dangling from a rope, came running towards his parents, who were relaxing on the porch sipping on some lemonade, and said,

"Mom ... Pop, look!" He shouted as he raced towards them, lifting the two rabbits above his head.

"What's that you have, son?" Lloyd asked with interest.

"My first catch, Pop." The lad beamed with youthful triumph. "Melvin taught me how." He was breathless and sweating by the time he stepped into the shade of the porch. "It took me months to master the art of making an effective trap, and Melvin said it takes a master hunter like his father was to be able to set effective traps." The youth babbled on. On the other hand, the couple exchanged a quick glance.

"Eh... what else did your young nigger teach you?" Sarah Davies asked.

"That a man is only a man if he can feed himself off the forest." Henry was wiping his brow with the back of his hand and had since laid the kill on the wooden floor.

"Oh, how nice," Sarah said. Then as an afterthought, she added, "Now, does the young nigger talk about not liking it here ... perhaps running off to some other plantation or living in the forest?"

"No, mama. In fact, he told me a lot about Kahuru. He's all he talks about."

"Ka what?"

"Kahuru, the human leopard, mom," Henry answered, not even for a moment suspecting that these were not simply idle questions asked on a hot Sunday afternoon.

"Oho ... some stupid folk tale," Lloyd said, trying to dismiss the subject.

"No, father it is true. The human leopard does exist. He saw him with his own eyes when he was back home."

Now, the couple was interested. Here was a slave trying to corrupt their ten-year-old son's thinking, their only son, who would one day inherit the plantation and continue where they left off. The warning of doom hung in the afternoon air like a hawk.

"Go to your room, and do your arithmetic, Henry," Lloyd ordered.

"But Papa, it's Sunday. All my work is done, and ..."

"Since when does your father have to tell you twice?" Sarah fumed.

Henry looked at his parents with genuine amazement. And without another word, he slowly picked up the two rabbits and dumped them in the kitchen sink before going up stairs to his room. His room faced the slave quarters down below. Something at the back of his mind told him that everything was not alright. His enthusiasm over the catch was somewhat dampened by his parents worried looks. Even at that tender age, he was old enough to recognize their various moods.

CHAPTER 7

MR. LLOYD DAVIES HAD TWO SLAVE overseers on his plantation, Wendell Phillips and Martin Duberman. Of the two, the most feared was Duberman, proud, ambitious, and persevering. He was also known to be artful, cruel, and bitter towards everything and everyone. He was the kind of man who could torture the slightest look, word, or gesture on the part of the salve into impudence and would treat it accordingly.

He would whip a slave to a pulp if he had reason to believe that the perpetrator had shown signs of laziness or insubordination. Duberman was notorious in all of Raymond, Mississippi, but Lloyd Davies always kept him on a tight leash, as unnecessary cruelty was something he did not tolerate. Before working for Lloyd Davies, Duberman was under a certain Benjamin James, who owned a tobacco plantation in northern Mississippi. He remained but a short time in the office of overseer. Why his career was short at the James plantation is not well known, but it was an open secret among the slaves that he had two murders hanging around his neck. The victims were slaves.

However, in a land where killing a slave or any other black person was no crime, whatsoever, there was never a formal investigation, let alone a hearing. So, when he worked under Lloyd Davies, life for him was sometimes very frustrating, because he could not be the slave driver he was capable of being. Lloyd Davies watched his every move like a hawk, and in some cases, encouraged slaves to report any unnecessary cruelty that they witnessed. But alas, no slave who worked the fields was brave enough to lodge a complaint, for they took Duberman's threats of retribution seriously.

In spite of all this, Martin Duberman walked around with a lot of anger and resentment in his heart. He was a volcano waiting to erupt. Thus, when Lloyd Davies came to him one day and asked him for a small favor, his eyes lit up. Martin Duberman had never felt so elated in ages. There was no assignment he would have taken with greater enthusiasm.

The task was simple; all he had to do was take a slave called Melvin Davies to the woods and "beat the African" out of him because Melvin was accused of corrupting the younger Davies' way of thinking. Melvin was filling his head with ideas of a mythical being named Kahuru, who was said to be half-man half-leopard.

Martin Duberman was to make certain that Melvin would never utter that name, again. This, Martin Duberman thought, was going to be cakewalk. He was going to inflict pain on the nigger slowly and surely, but altogether, very thoroughly.

The morning was chilly when Duberman stormed into the slave quarters. This was routine, for everybody was up and ready by the time the door slammed behind him.

"Melvin!" He shouted. "Get up and get the mules and the wagon ready. You and I are going to the creek for some wood." The creek was at the grove, five miles northeast of the plantation.

"Yes, master." Sanza said as he rubbed his eyes and stretched his limbs.

"Come now, boy. I ain't got all day boy. Move your black hide." The veins on his sunburned neck were bulging blue.

Sanza was already at the door and trotting towards the barn. He yoked the two mules and was ready by the time Duberman arrived. They headed out in silence, Sanza carrying an ax and driving the mules with Duberman following close by on his horse.

Upon reaching the grove, Sanza immediately went to work. He began by chopping down several trees and arranging them in neat piles before loading them on the wagon. It was a tedious and strenuous job. Before long, his stomach began to rumble, and his arms felt like lead, but he did not stop until he was ready.

He wiped his flushed brow with the back of his palm and looked at the overseer, who was pleasantly munching at a meat sandwich.

"Why are you eye-balling me, boy?" Duberman asked with naked contempt and suspicion as he wiped the corners of his mouth.

"I am sorry sir, but work is done, and ..."

"I say when it's done, boy."

"But Master Duberman, if there is any more that I can do, please tell me what it is." This time, he avoided eye contact but looked instead, at the musket the overseer was brandishing.

"And since when does a worthless nigger talk back to me?" Duberman laid the weapon on the wagon, a most relieving sight, and took a menacing step towards the slave. He was of medium height and build, but not very strong, as Sanza had observed long ago at the fields.

"I mean no disrespect to you, master, but is there any more work to do?" This time, he made eye contact with the overseer.

"Oho, so you are that smart storytelling nigger, who fills little Henry's head about some stupid phantom, eh?"

He looked like he was going to attack Sanza. Upon observing this, the latter took a step backwards.

"No, he is no phantom." Duberman's words had stung him.

"I beg your pardon, boy?" The overseer was closing in.

"Kahuru, the human leopard, does exist. I have seen that remarkable warrior with these very two eyes."

An assault was imminent. It happened almost immediately after the thought flashed through his mind. A vicious blow to his face split his lower lip, and Sanza thought he felt two premolars dislodge as he staggered a few paces back.

Duberman came rushing at him, but what the overseer did not know was that he was up against someone who, at one point in his life, had been a budding wrestling champion. Sanza assumed the proper stance and came to grips with his assailant.

He stooped low and carried Duberman on his right shoulder before flinging him hard on his back to the ground. The impact knocked the wind out of Duberman's lungs. Sanza waited for him to get up. He knew, too well, the consequences of striking a white man but had since thrown caution to the wind.

Upon recovering from the shock, Martin Duberman, red with fury, sprang like a wounded buffalo and threw himself headfirst at the slave, aiming for the head, but the latter stepped aside and watched him hit the turf. This time, he did not wait for him to get up but instead, flung himself unto his body.

For a while, the two struggled with one another like two mad cobras, each wondering (as their muscles took the strain) which move would be effective for their current positions. It looked like a fight to the death, with no man willing to give in just yet. Duberman tried poking his fingernails into Sanza's eyes, but the latter was too quick, eluding the assault and countering with blows to the face.

The two rolled towards the creek, and before long, it was a question of stamina—who was going to outlast the other. Before reaching the water, Sanza managed, with ease, to halt their momentum with one knee and continue pounding Duberman's face with his fists.

By this time, Duberman was putting up little or no resistance. As a final humiliation, Sanza decided to stuff his mouth with sand. As he was about to reach out for a handful, Duberman heaved his trunk sideways; this made Sanza change his mind and instead, lift the overseer above his head and toss him into the creek like a bag of corn.

Both of their faces were covered with blood as Martin Duberman's body hit the bottom of the shallow creek, the cold water reviving him, and Sanza followed with a war cry that brought back memories he had tried so hard to suppress over the seasons. As he waded towards Duberman, he saw the two men who broke into his hut and kidnapped him as a child many seasons ago. He remembered Masamba's treachery; he saw the long journey through the dense forest and its dread, he saw the body of Nzimbi thrown into a pit, his feverish body at the mercy of a deadly cobra, and he saw the face of Kahuru, the leopard man.

He was bound on finishing the job by drowning the overseer, but instead, he pulled him by the collar of his shirt and dragged him ashore. It took a while for the two to catch their breath.

"Master Duberman," Sanza said. "Contrary to what anybody has told you, Kahuru, the leopard man, does exist. I saw him with these two very eyes."

It took a while for the statement to sink in, and when it did, the slave overseer, Martin Duberman's (reduced now to a mere mortal) answer was:

"Yes, maybe … your conviction is proof enough."

Sanza was a bit surprised. He knew how proud Duberman was, and for him to swallow his pride and somewhat believe a story like that from a slave was unheard of. Or, there was a much more logical explanation; Duberman was reaching into his human side.

"What do we do now, sir?" Sanza asked.

"First," Duberman said, still panting, "this incident never happened. I hear one word of it from anyone, even Mr. Davies …" He brandished his musket.

"I will blow that nigger head off your shoulders."

Sanza knew this was no empty threat, not to say he was afraid of him or scared of death; the reputation of this man's disdain for black people preceded him.

"But why attack me, Master Duberman? What did I do?"

"You are not going to continue telling stories to the young Davies about your human leopard. The boy believes so much of that mumbo jumbo already that his parents are scared that sooner or later, he may not be able to tell fact from fantasy," he said.

"But, Master Duberman, what I told the young master is the truth. It came about when he asked me to teach him how to catch rabbits. You see, where I come from, lying is considered as bad as stealing." Duberman, once again, did not fail to notice the absolute conviction in his voice.

He looked at Sanza for a while. There was some blood trickling from his lower lip and a small bruise on his forehead, but it was the overseer who looked no less worse for the wear and tried his best to make his face look more presentable by constantly rubbing the lumps on his forehead.

"Who taught you how to fight?"

"The Bamongo people, whose village is no more (from what I can remember) after it was burned to the ground, following the war."

"They taught you how to fight?"

"Yes, I was destined to be their wrestling champion, had it not been for my capture," Sanza boasted as he unconsciously flexed his knotted biceps.

"And this Kahuru, was he a wrestler, too?"

"No, Kahuru was a warrior sent from the ancestors and the gods to bring about peace and goodwill in the land. No one knows exactly who created him, but he was well-known throughout the land and beyond for his might and bravery." Sanza would have kept on talking for the rest of his life if given the chance to retell Kahuru's deeds.

"And you say you saw him?" It looked like Duberman was warming up to this somewhat tall tale.

"Yes, sir! With these two very eyes. I was but a boy then, a little younger than little master Davies. I had been kidnapped from my father's house by a fellow villager named Masamba Kali to be sold off into slavery." He had told that story so often that by now, he no longer felt the chocking lump in his throat.

"So, your own people do practice slavery?" This was fascinating to Martin Duberman, a staunch believer in slavery although small movements of people in the North were beginning to speak openly against it. These people were known as "Abolitionists," a word Duberman was not quite familiar with but at the same time, did not like.

"Yes, there are nations back home that have slaves. However, these slaves are not snatched from their homes but are mainly prisoners of war or are given by someone repaying an outstanding debt. The people who kidnapped collaborated with the Arabs."

"Arabs? What kind of people are they?"

"White or almost white like you. They needed slaves to carry the ivory through the thick forests for them, and the captives were heard from no more."

Sanza had already yoked the mules, once again, an indication that he was ready to depart if his overseer was.

"These Arabs, according to my father," he continued "believed so much in the ivory they got from these tusks that it was little wonder that they have been known to our people for over two hundred seasons."

"You mean years," Duberman corrected.

"Whatever you call a season in this land."

Martin Duberman simply nodded. He was impressed; no doubt this indeed, was a smart nigger, he thought. He recalled details with crystal clear accuracy. No wonder Lloyd Davies had somewhat of a soft spot for him because if it had been any other slave, he would have been dead long ago. The last thing a slave owner wanted was a "smart ass," as they were known. They were the type that most certainly caused trouble.

Sanza was different, though; not only was he strong and hard-working, but he was also intelligent, obedient, and unassuming. It was a pity, according to Duberman, that he was born black. Otherwise, he would have been somebody on God's green earth. Martin Duberman only hated him and all others because of the color of their skin.

"Well, Melvin," he said at last, "it's time for us to be heading back, and like I said, no more stories to the young Davies about the human leopard."

"Yes, sir." Sanza said, as he began driving the mules back home.

That night, Sanza lay awake on his bed, which was the hard, cold floor cushioned with hay. The night was chilly, so he had on two extra blankets. At first, that was the thing about this strange land he did not understand,. There were times in the season when the weather would suddenly become unbearably cold, especially when the white flakes, which he quickly learned to be snow, fell from the sky.

He was falling asleep when he heard soft footsteps tiptoeing towards him. His insides knotted as he sat up, reaching with his right hand for a club from within a confused network of hay kept underneath him mainly for one purpose. That purpose was to ward off any unexpected attack.

"Melvin," A shrill voice called out quietly in the dark.

"Master Davies... I mean, little master Davies, is that you?"

"Yes," Henry Davies said as he sat next to Sanza, who had quickly and unobtrusively stashed the weapon in its sanctuary.

"What are you doing here? You know I could get into a lot of trouble." He was right.

"Don't worry. I snuck out, and nobody will notice because I'll sneak back in again." The younger Davies was dressed in white, long john cotton pajamas.

"Good. Now you better get back before somebody sees you."

"Not until you tell me more about Kahuru, the human leopard."

"It's too late for that, little master. Besides, I am supposed to tell you nothing about Kahuru." Inside, he was dying to start talking. The legend of Kahuru was the only thing he had in him that helped him withstand all the blows life threw at him since he was kidnapped from his hut in what seemed like a lifetime ago.

"Melvin, I am not leaving until I hear more," the young Davies was adamant.

"Are you sure you want to hear this, little master?"

"Certainly, why do you think I am here?"

"Aright then, for the next two nights, we will be meeting here at the same time…."

"Why?" was the interrupting question.

"Because that's how long it will take to tell you all I know about this remarkable being. I will be like a chronicler, so please don't interrupt me, as this will help me recall the names of places and people much easier."

Sanza sat up and sighed. This was followed by a long silence. Then Henry coughed. As if in answer, an owl hard by gave vent to a long eerie hoot. The sound died in a hair-raising *diminuendo*. Thus, on that chilly night of 1779, on a plantation in Raymond, Mississippi, the deeds of Kahuru, the human leopard, would be retold to an audience of one. And little did they know that this tale and the subsequent, clandestine meetings were to drastically change the life of Henry Thomas Davies later on.

PART 2: SOUTHERN AFRICA 1772

CHAPTER 8

THE GREAT DRAKENSBERG MOUNTAINS in Southern Africa overlooked the land of the Bakhudung, the land of never-ending jubilation and the land of peace and tranquility. It was the land of fierce and brave warriors, and it was from this land that Kahuru, the human leopard, is believed to have originated.

The village of the Bakhudung lay in the plains, amidst a thick forest. There were hundreds of beehive huts surrounding an arena, which handled the day-to-day activities of the village. These people were under the stern leadership of King Swathi, the son of Muata, a man of wisdom and courage known to many as "The Lion." What signified his kingship was a necklace around his neck with crocodile teeth dangling from it.

The story of Kahuru is this: Many seasons earlier, a village Great's wife put to bed a bouncing baby boy, whom they named Tladi—lightning. From an early age, his father, Ndaba, the poet and orator, noticed that the boy showed signs of valor and wisdom well beyond his age. This same observation was not lost among the villagers, and everybody agreed that Tladi was a special child, and they were right. Tladi grew up to be a great warrior and hunter and was destined for greatness.

At the tender age of eighteen, he was assigned commander of his regiment, comprised of boys his age group who had just recently been initiated into manhood. On top of this, Tladi was also named among the village Greats; men of virtue and men who had solid personal achievements to their credit. This feat was unprecedented for someone his age. This was when Lindiwe, the village beauty and also the most desirable girl, fell in love with the young warrior and declared herself solely to him.

But alas! This bred resentment in some of his peers, one of them a young man by the name of Makopela, to be exact, the son of Monwabisi. Like Tladi, he was an awesome warrior, but he lacked Tladi's intelligence, grace, and agility. What Makopela had was physical strength, and some elders had even remarked that he had the best pair of knotted biceps in the village, that is, of course, if they excluded Tladi.

However, Makopela had one fault amongst many, which the villagers disliked. He was jealous, self-seeking, and still worse, he had a temper like a man with whitlows on all ten fingers. Thus, it was no surprise that he felt overlooked when Tladi was chosen leader of their regiment and when Lindiwe had become the woman in his life.

Makopela then decided to deal with his rival. This he did with the help of two of his closest friends, Njenje and Haru. Their intention was to murder the young warrior while he was on one of his hunting missions. The attack was swift and sudden in the depths of the primeval forest. Tladi's face was deformed by a highly poisoned spear, and he was left for dead.

Although Tladi survived this assault, his life changed considerably. His features were grotesque, and many a people shunned him. Out of desperation, Tladi left the village and was never heard from for many seasons. Only Lindiwe, the village beauty, guarded the secret of the ill-fated youth's disappearance. Tladi had ventured to a land where no one had dared to set foot.

Tladi headed eastwards through the forest, across the plains and canyons, to the dreaded mountains where a sorcerer by the name of Zebe was said to have dwelt. Tladi met this strange man, who in fact, was an oracle with powers beyond imagination. He told the young warrior about a great evil that was soon to happen and said that Tladi, himself, was chosen by the gods and the ancestors to bring about peace and goodwill in the land and beyond.

Amidst frightful happenings that lack proper description, Zebe, the oracle of Good, transformed Tladi into Kahuru, the master of all men and beast.

A strange metamorphosis had occurred. The young warrior turned into a half-man half-leopard. His whole body was covered with soft, dark fur, his teeth turned into canines and carnassials, and the ears assumed an almost triangular shape. Whiskers that moved benevolently shot out, and so did a tail, just above his buttocks. His hands turned into claws that still maintained their human mechanism. His feet acquired a similar revolution. He was also enormous and muscular, capable of taking ten strong men and beasts at one encounter with ease.

Also given to him by the oracle, was the famous magic spear, which upon striking its target, would disengage and fly back to its owner's hand. The aim of this magnificent weapon was said to be true and never faltering. There were five leopards assigned to him in order to watch his back when engaged in full-fledged combat, and these animals were an asset to Kahuru, as later events would dictate.

A great calamity hit the land as Zebe had predicted. An army of warlike outcasts emerged, led by the crafty and blood-thirsty Makopela. After it was discovered that the attack on Tladi was Makopela's handiwork, Makopela and his two partners in crime fled the village, never to return. They lived in the forest and became hardened savages. It was also during this time that Makopela dreamt of ultimate power in the land until it became a burning obsession.

By the time they were ready to wreak havoc, Makopela and his brigands had risen to an army of well over ten thousand men. Their hiding place was deep in the heart of the forest at a formidable fortress known as Khotsong—the place of peace. This army of outcasts attacked and destroyed so many villages in their path that before long, they became a force to be reckoned with.

It was during this peak of Makopela's might that all major villages decided to join forces and form a unified army whose sole purpose was to squash Makopela's army once and for all and hence, end his deadly campaign of terror. Kahuru, the human leopard, King Swathi of the Bakhudung, and King Morobe of the Bafokeng were the chosen commanders of this army.

Following a great battle, which is still talked about today, the unified army prevailed. Makopela, himself, was captured together with a few who managed to escape, and they were executed. The final quest of Kahuru had been realized.

The big question remained, though, after peace was restored. Who was Kahuru? True, he came from the mountains, but that was nowhere as far as everybody was concerned. Even Kahuru, himself, wanted to know his true identity. There were certain things that happened to him, for which he found no logic explanation. He felt certain that there were people and things he knew, perhaps from a previous life, one of them being the village beauty known as Lindiwe.

There was only one key to this mystery, and that of course, was Zebe, the oracle and the divine sorcerer of Good. The leopard man had, on one occasion, asked the oracle who he really was. This was before the former was about to embark on a mission deep into the interior to quell a marauding gorilla. It was on this same journey that Sanza Kazadi was to see, with his own eyes, this great phenomenon.

Upon asking the oracle about his true identity, Zebe is said to have replied Kahuru:

"You will know the truth one day. That is not important now. What I ask of you, now, is to go and prepare for your forthcoming venture. May the force of Good be with you."

Now the time had come, and this happened one moon after the fall of Makopela and his army. The oracle summoned Swathi and a few members from the council of elders including Ndaba, the poet and orator. This he did by visiting the men in their dreams. Upon arriving at the mountains, they witnessed Zebe transform Kahuru back into Tladi, the young warrior who had been lost to the village for seasons.

There was great joy when the announcement was made to the village the next morning. The whole village gathered at the royal hut, and the young warrior was dramatically revealed. A feast was prepared, which ran days on end. Merrymaking and joy became a way of life. The rains fell so hard that season that the fertile lands produced more than anyone could remember. Not even the oldest member of the village could recall so much joy and abundance.

Things went on like that for a while. The men still worked hard at the fields, and food and game were in such great abundance that before long, people had forgotten the calamity and terror that had gripped the land only two seasons earlier. And it was at this time, that another blow was to strike again. It began like a single drop that eventually turns into a waterfall. That single drop began in the form of four brothers, the sons of Pongoza, a village Great, and this drop was subsequently followed by a major invasion.

CHAPTER 9

PONGOZA, THE SON OF MAGWAZA, was such a
magnificent warrior that before long, he was given
the title of Great. This was similar in title to the
English knighthood. This title exempted him,
thereafter, from active duty in the army and
allowed him to marry. He then fathered five
children.

Of the five, four were boys, who came in rapid
succession and who he decided to groom to
greatness when they became men. As it turned out,
the four boys, Zweli, Mbateni, Shandu, and Dala,
were nothing near what their father was or even
what he had hoped they would become. They
grew up to be lazy, disobedient, and incorrigible.
Many times, Pongoza would warn them of their
impending doom if they carried on with their
ways, but all his words fell on deaf ears.

There were times when he would mercilessly
employ the whip with the hope that they would
maybe recant their ways, but this only seemed to
strengthen their resolve to carry out their wayward
behaviors. It was as if they had grown immune to
the pain the stick inflicted. There was only one

thing to do and that was to bring forth this matter before Swathi and the council of elders. It was common, in those days, to seek this kind of counsel when it came to family affairs. This form of appeal was only made if it looked certain that a particular problem was getting out of hand, as it was in this instance.

Thus, one early morning, Pongoza walked into the royal hut and found the king and council of elders already waiting. He offered the necessary greetings and sat down on a stool that was facing the king and the council, who were seated in a semi-circular arrangement. Pongoza looked around the hut. It was enormous and well decorated with numerous beads, magnificent animal skins, and figures of the king's forefathers hanging from the walls. The interior would have been dark, even in broad daylight, had it not been for the smokeless fire in the middle of the room that seemed to burn eternally.

The veteran warrior noiselessly cleared his throat before speaking.

"Swathi, the great king, son of Muata of the swamps, a man of wisdom, courage, and strength, I, your humble servant and subject, come before you and this great council with what may seem as a small issue, but one that may manifest into something much larger."

"Speak up, son of Magwaza," the king said encouragingly. "Speak, for that's why we are here—to make right what may be wrong."

The rest of the elders nodded in agreement.

"I have but one problem, and that problem is my children."

They all knew what the problem was beforehand.

"As you know, great king and respectable elders," Pongoza continued. "All my sons have been initiated into manhood." This meant they were over the age of eighteen. "But they are hardly men a father can be proud of. They do not have fields they can call their own nor do they have any livestock. They will not hunt, nor will they tend to the family flock. I have heard complaints from the leader of their regiment that they have become insubordinate. It fills me with dread to think what will become of my compound and cattle after I am gone. My children are disappearing right before my eyes, like a rock of salt underwater. Please, great king, I implore you. These children belong to the village as much as they belong to me."

The silence was deafening as soon as the last statement was driven home. This was not a matter to be taken lightly. Just seasons earlier, a young warrior named Makopela had fled the village with two accomplices and built an army of outcasts, who at this very moment, were threatening king Swathi's throne.

"Bring the boys before me in one moon. I would deal with them now, but we have a more pressing issue at hand, as you will soon know."

The "pressing issue at hand" that the king had talked about, was the impending war with the outcasts. But alas! It was in this war that Pongoza, son of Magwaza, fell. The[†] veteran warrior was given a state funeral, and shortly after, the king was so overwhelmed by domestic issues—the arrival of a long-lost son of the village and warrior Tladi being one of them—that in time, Swathi forgot about Pongoza's plea until the matter got completely out of hand.

Shortly after their father's death, the four youth's behavior left much to be desired. Their fields were overrun, and they developed rude manners. Their appearance became loathsome. Nobody could tell what their problem was. Some said the brothers were at the mercy of a wicked spell, in other words, they were bewitched, but by whom and why?

What they did not have, they took. Simply put, they became thieves of the night, a practice that was alien among the Bakhudung. Consequently,

---

[†] In this war, as a matter of state emergency, even the Greats were called to active duty in the army.

they were always quarreling with neighbors over land, livestock, and other such things. That was when king Swathi remembered Pongoza's plea and intervened.

After being summoned to the royal hut, the four brothers found themselves standing before the king and his council, one early morning. The air was cold, as there was a steady breeze that came from the snow-capped Drakensberg. The four brothers stood in silence, each wondering what the king had in store for them. Following the usual custom, Swathi spoke up:

"Young men, close to six moons ago, your father came before us to complain about your disturbing behavior. That was just before the war with the outcasts at Khotsong, and as we all know, that great warrior, who was your father, fell like the true Great he was." The king eyed the youth with a kind of gaze that seemed to look through them. He was tall and well-built; a man who had seen a lot in his lifetime. "Therefore, I ask you, Zweli, in particular, since you are the oldest and should be leading by example. Why, just tell me why you have to desecrate your father's good name by resorting to this kind of behavior?"

The eldest of the brothers merely stared at the king, his tongue stuck to the roof of his mouth. The brothers were a few moons apart in age, so that's why they all stood at almost the same height.

"And you," the king continued, "Mbateni and Shandu, I've heard of people's goats missing. You know our laws against stealing. Why do you make the name of the Bakhudung stink?"

Although the king was asking the youth questions, they were not to answer or say anything in their defense. What Swathi was doing was merely stating facts in the form of questions.

"Dala," Swathi's venom was now directed at the youngest of the brothers. "Our nation cannot afford to see another youth go to waste and worse, end up like Makopela and company. Is it true that you tried to force yourself unto the daughter of Malepa?"

This time, the king demanded an answer, for this was a very serious charge. Dala, the youngest of the four, grazed the sole of his foot on the ground before answering, an obvious sign of nervousness. In a barely audible voice, he said,

"It is not exactly as the king has heard. The daughter of Malepa had consented to my advances and …"

"Stop!" Monaheng interjected, almost shouting. He was the king's chief advisor. "What do you think this is, eh? One of the games you children play? What you did goes against Bakhudung culture and ethics. It is an abomination and an insult to our ancestors and the good name of your father." Only he had the prerogative to throw in his word before being asked to in matters such as these.

"Anyway," the king continued calmly despite Monaheng's brief outburst. "This kind of behavior is going to end. You will work the fields and tend to your flock. You shall be more responsible, and to ensure that, I shall designate fifty of the finest royal cattle under your care. For the next six moons, you are to tend to them. Take them grazing, and make sure they are back in the kraal by dusk. I will not lose a single cow during this tenure, but instead, I will expect to see five cows to be heavy with child. And to ensure this, my prize-winning bull will be among the cattle under your care."

Some of the elders, including Monaheng, winced when they heard the last statement. The prize-winning, sacred bull the king talked about was special and a wonder to the villagers because of its mating capability. It never left the royal kraal because it produced the best heifers in the village.

"Now," Swathi continued. "If there is any lax in your duty for the next six moons, even once, your punishment will be most severe. I will see you first thing in the morning. Be off."

The four young men left without a word. They were extremely relieved to say the least. Shortly after they left, Monaheng waited until they were completely out of hearing range and said,

"Great king, and I say this with respect, it is a grave mistake to entrust those boys with any of the royal cattle, especially the sacred bull."

"True to word, Monaheng, but entrusting these boys with that responsibility will do more good than harm. When one tries to be harsh, they rebel, and when they rebel, bad things are bound to happen. Remember those accursed youths, Makopela, Njenje, and Haru?"

Who would ever forget?

"But those youths were bewitched, great king. This is a totally isolated issue." It was Mophosho, the sub-chief, who spoke this time. He also happened to be the father of Lindiwe, the village beauty.

"I agree, Mophosho, but I think we owe it to their father to be a little lenient with them. Pongoza was a great warrior, and his deeds should not be forgotten," the king said with finality, and there was no arguing with this line of reasoning.

Thereafter, following other trivial issues concerning the village, the meeting was adjourned. However, a date was set for another meeting. This was meant to further assess the progress of the four youth.

For the next three moons, the children of Pongoza adhered to their duties. They attended to their flock and the king's flock and ploughed the land. They were up at the first cockcrow and were in the forest to graze the herd by dawn, making certain that the cattle grazed the finest pastures, and in doing this, they were very diligent, very careful not to invoke the wrath of king Swathi, who at times sent spies to unobtrusively observe the lads. The reports that came back were very encouraging and always the same. The brothers were doing a fine job. Their lands were beginning to blossom and bear fruit, and their personal flock, including that of the king's, was showing signs of multiplying rapidly in the not too distant future.

The king and the council watched these transformations with joy and fascination. They all unanimously agreed that the brothers had passed the most difficult phase of their life. It seemed too good to be true, such that after a while, the grip Swathi had on them somewhat slackened a bit. And that was when the blow struck again. The four brother's eccentricities, which had been kept at bay for some time, suddenly became dangerously active.

The lads became even more irresponsible. They began by neglecting their fields, once more. The cattle that had been assigned under their care would suddenly stray dangerously away from sight while they played in the river and roasted game all day. Dala resumed pursuing girls whenever the opportunity presented itself. Some said his loins did his thinking for him.

Then, on one fateful day, the brothers were engaged in their daily activity of roasting rabbit meat and swimming, when a man-eater (a lion that ceases to hunt due to old age) pounced from nowhere and attacked the royal cattle, killing three in the process including the king's sacred bull.

When the news reached the king, a small regiment was dispatched to apprehend the erring youths and bring them before Swathi. The raid was so swift and surprising that the members of this particular regiment were in time to witness the most heinous social offences ever known in Bakhudung code. Dala was found sleeping with his youngest sister who at the time, was barely eleven seasons old.

Without much resistance, the youth were arrested. When brought before Swathi, they were all charged with the crime. Following a mass ritual in which the young girl was cleansed, the brothers were brought forth before the entire village. The news had sent such ripples of shockwaves in the land and beyond that it still is, to some members of the Bakhudung, considered an abomination to retell that foul deed.

The brothers, Zweli, Mbateni, Shandu, and Dala, were considered worse than outcasts. Never had people heard of such an infamous act. The final straw had landed, and the king dealt them one of the harshest sentences ever known. They were banished from the village forever. The compound that had once belonged to a Great was burned to the ground.

Amidst all these happenings, King Swathi could only deduce that these were the makings of a bad omen. Little did he know that this was just the beginning. The youth would later be known as the vulture brothers, who terrorized hunters far and beyond.

CHAPTER 10

SWATHI'S INFLUENCE STRETCHED beyond the borders of the Bakhudung into far off lands. Since his word was law and he had a strong army and people behind him, many nations swore allegiance to him. In return, they had his protection. To ensure that they had his protection on a regular basis; the clans paid tribute to him seasonally and without delay or any compunction.

Every once in a while, Swathi would dispatch a handpicked delegation of twenty of the best and toughest warriors. Their mission was to travel to these far-off lands, collect rewards that were entitled to the king, and also, attend to the grievances these chiefs might have. In some cases, this meant serious crimes like murder or treason. Swathi, a man who always believed in nipping a problem in the bud before it manifested, would have the offenders brought before him and tried. In time, Swathi and his council of elders became the highest form of court in the land.

Also, if there was a village faced with a major threat like invasion, for example, Swathi would be notified immediately, and a huge number of the

Bakhudung warriors would be dispatched, and in time, the thereat would be quelled.

One morning, the leader of such a delegation that would be sent to far off villages was summoned to the royal hut. His name was Mapoulo. He was tough, resilient, and wise, as one might expect for the leader of this elite unit. Mapoulo was clad in full war gala, as he knew he was about to lead yet another mission.

"Great king," Mapoulo bowed cordially upon entering the king's massive hut.

The morning was cold. Swathi was seated on the sacred stool, flanked by two of his most personal guards and some members of the great council of elders. As usual, there was a large, smokeless fire in the middle of the room.

The warrior knelt on the spotless floor and faced the ground. The fire was between him and the king.

"Mapoulo," the king's booming voice seemed to be coming from the very walls of the hut. "You are to set off immediately to the land of the Barolong in the deep north; there has been a distress call."

"Consider it done, great king." Mapoulo concurred, still facing the floor; a sign of great respect for his king.

"This time, you are to lead the second-generation Buffalo regiment." For the first time, Mapoulo raised his head and faced the king. This was an unusual assignment. The Buffalo regiment comprised of youth between the ages of eighteen and twenty. These were young men, who were known for their relentless fighting spirit and agility. The forthcoming mission was certainly no routine patrol of the neighboring clans. Something more drastic was at hand. The warrior wondered what it was, but knew he was about to find out.

"Last night, two of Moabi's (the Barolong king) fastest runners arrived. They came to address a grave concern." The king paused and looked at Mapoulo for a while before continuing. "One of their clansmen had been herding his cattle two days walk away from their village, when suddenly, he saw in the northeastern horizon, a thick cloud of dust, the type of dust that is caused by thousands of men on a hard march, men big in size and in feet to cause such a disturbance to be seen as far as the eye can see."

For the first time in his life, Mapoulo felt the type of fear that made his armpits itch and sweat. If the king was saying what he thought he was going to say, then peace and human kind, as they knew it, was soon to be a memory once cherished.

"The witness to that event ran for two days and nights, stopping only when he collapsed in front of

Moabi's compound and crawled on his belly, with only a few words coming from his dying lips." Right here, the king stopped, and following the dramatic pause, the witness said, "The Tompiki are coming."

Mapoulo almost fell to the floor. His head started spinning as though he was falling into a dark and bottomless hole. His mouth dried up as he felt fear rise from the basin of his stomach. It tasked his entire manliness not to show it, but he knew just like everyone else in that room that day that this was no ordinary threat they were about to encounter.

"What you must do is assemble the Buffalo regiment and head on out to the land of the Barolong. Observe from a safe distance and see if indeed, it is the Tompiki the villager saw. Meanwhile, we will make the necessary preparations for a possible invasion." Swathi sighed and wiped the tiny beads of sweat on his brow. He, too, had been equally shaken by the news.

At last, Mapoulo rose, after bowing one more time to the king, and said,

"It will be done as the great king known as the lion commands." And he was gone.

Back at the royal hut, there was a long silence before Swathi cleared his throat and looked around at the other men seated with him. His chair, known as "the sacred stool," was high above the floor, making him tower over everybody else like the king he was. Among the council and a few Greats, was Ndaba, the poet and orator, father of one of the most elite and bravest warriors the Bakhudung have ever known—Tladi.

A meeting of this magnitude was employed only in very serious situations such as a loss of a man in the forest, murder, and invasion. But this time, the men were about to explore into a great village secret that began many seasons before.

"If, indeed, it is the Tompiki we are up against, then the spirit of Kahuru will have to be revived." It was just like Swathi not to mince his words with suitable parables when faced with a possible crisis. There was an audible reaction of shock when this statement was delivered.

"Great king," it was Monaheng, the chief advisor, who spoke this time. "We promised the great oracle and sorcerer known as Zebe that we will never bring forth such a request."

The other men nodded in agreement. Only Ndaba, the poet and orator, was silent. His arms were folded on his chest as if he was someone reserving his opinion.

"If I recall correctly, it was the gods and the forces of Good that created Kahuru to bring about peace and goodwill. We need his help again," Swathi countered.

"But what if there is no invasion. What good will it do to revive Kahuru?" It was the old man, Thulani, who spoke this time.

"Men of the Bakhudung, you saw those messengers last night. Who in their right minds would travel that great distance to report such a happening if they were not certain, themselves?" The king asked, and before anybody could answer, he continued, "Listen, people. You all know that we have the strongest army known to men; few nations would dare to stand in our path. However, this is a threat from another world, the secret, harsh world beyond the horizon. From what we've heard from our days as children, we will need more than our mortal strength to fight the Tompiki; we need Kahuru."

The rest of the men were silent for a while. What the king said made a lot of sense, but they were faced with a problem. Kahuru was a closely guarded state secret. Only the men present knew his human identity, and that was none other than Tladi, the son of Ndaba the poet and orator. If Kahuru were to reappear, then Tladi would have to disappear. The villagers would have to be given an explanation about this rare coincidence, something the five men in that royal hut had hoped never to face in their lifetime.

The truth of the matter is that if it became common knowledge that Kahuru was Tladi's alter ego, then the young man's life would be in danger. Even though the outcasts had been annihilated, there was no telling who the other enemies might be, especially if that kind of enemy was the silent type—the type that smiled in your face. An attempt had once been made on the young Great's life. Another attempt was likely to succeed where the first had failed.

Following the long, uncomfortable silence, the old man, Thulani, cleared his throat and spoke,

"It is as the king speaks. It is always wise to prepare for danger even when there is none to prepare for. If, indeed, it is the Tompiki coming, then we must be ready for them."

"I agree," it was Mophosho, the sub chief, who spoke this time.

"So do I," said Ndaba, the poet and orator.

"Then it is settled. Issue an order to bring forth the son of Ndaba at once and mobilize our entire army. They should be ready within fifteen days," the king ordered. The men stood up as quickly as their old, quacking bones would let them, bowing in their cordial, traditional way at the king and wishing him strength, long life, and more wisdom as they filed out of the royal hut.

Now, who were the Tompiki? Many seasons ago, when King Swathi was still a boy, five men from the Bakhudung nation went on a journey into the deep north of the land. These were men whose lives were dedicated to traveling into far off lands, their sole mission to study the ways of life of other nations in foreign lands and to bring back what they had learned in order to share it with their people. These men were known as the *Batsamai*— the travelers.

On this particular journey; the five men decided to venture where no man in their clan had set foot. For days and nights, these men walked— encountering unspeakable dangers on the way. After almost two seasons, they crossed the great river (the Zambezi). It was here that they encountered the Batonka people, men who build their villages upon the shores of the great river (they still do). Their villages are always temporal as they must follow the migrations of shoals of Tilapia, Tiger Fish, and Barbeled Catfish, on which they live.

It was through these people, that the travelers came to know about the Tompiki. To this day, nobody knows where these people originated, only that they were people with unusual, if not frightening, features. The average Tompiki man stood over six feet five inches (over two meters), so they were known as a race of giants. "*Hard men with faces of lions,"* as the chief of the Batonka put it.

They were a nomadic people, who wreaked havoc in their paths and left the land bare like a multitude of locusts. There had always been a nagging fear that these people would one day invade the land of the Bakhudung. According to the travelers, two of whom survived that journey, the Tompiki were herding south. The Tompiki were also known for making slaves out of nations who would brave their attack, and thereafter, leaving them to the mercy of hunger after they sucked the land dry.

Many songs and stories were composed about these strange people, but when told to children, it was said the Tompiki were a race of elves, who stood at the same height as the human index finger. It is not clear, now, what really happened to the three men who did not make it back to the village, but it is strongly believed that they fell victim to the Tompiki. But, the man who lived to tell this story did, in fact, encounter these strange beings.

It was while they were still enjoying the hospitality of the Batonka when, one day, the alarm was raised by one of the village sentries. He had seen these men coming. Not being a warlike people, the chief ordered everybody to retreat down river. They were just in time to board their canoes and flow with the current of the Zambezi when, in the distance, the Tompiki arrived at the recently deserted village. Shortly thereafter, thick dark smoke was visible, indicating that the giants were engaged in what they did best, looting and scrounging at the empty village.

For three days and nights, the entire Batonka flotilla cruised along with the flow of the great river. It was only when they felt that they were far from harm's way that they decided to dock and erect yet another settlement. Apart from those who were unfortunate to have their canoes capsized by hippopotamuses, every man, woman, and child was accounted for.

Everyone except three of the five travelers from the Bakhudung had survived. The Batonka chief later on explained that was how they almost always succeeded at eluding the bloodthirsty Tompiki, by escaping on canoe before the marauders reached their village. And this they did by setting up their village close to the river and posting sentries at strategic positions. But he went on to say that in his lifetime, he had twice witnessed his village taken by complete surprise and few escaping with their lives.

The two remaining *Batsamai*, Gazi and Sokhulu, thanked the Batonka and their chief for their hospitality and above all, for saving their lives before beginning their long journey back home. They passed by a great sight, moons later, where the river turned into a great waterfall, creating a scene of breathtaking wonder. The local folk they met called this place "where the smoke thunders," *"mosi oa thunya."* But, these two travelers knew it simply as "the place of never-ending beauty." Gazi lived to be a hundred and twenty-two seasons, and the last words from his dying lips were:

"I thank the ancestors and the gods that I lived to tell my children, grandchildren, and great grandchildren that I saw a place where smoke thunders."

Another traveler, from a land far off land about a hundred seasons later, would appreciate the same view and name it "Victoria Falls" in honor of his queen, the queen of England.[‡]

And that is how the Bakhudung knew the Tompiki, and it was sixty seasons later that the threat was to knock at their doorstep and that the half-man half-leopard known as Kahuru was to reemerge after a long absence.

[‡] This was the explorer, missionary, and doctor David Livingston.

CHAPTER 11

DEEP IN THE PRIMEVAL FOREST, Tladi contemplated his situation. He was sitting on a rock, and at his feet, was a beige antelope, striped with pale chalk lines across its back with long legs, a long neck, and huge trumpet-shaped ears. One could see it was male because of its wide, corkscrew horns. The eyes were wide open but stared at nothing.

It was another great kill for a great hunter but one he would not so easily forget. He had begun stalking this animal two days before, but unlike a gemsbok, an antelope is much more elusive. It kept the distance between them at a little over a spear throw. This meant that, even with his amazing spear throwing capability, there was nothing this great, young warrior and hunter could do. He would have to await his chance. Patience was a hunter and warrior's single most important virtue.

On the third day, his food supply was running low, and he knew any attempt to replenish it might give his quarry the chance to escape from his sight. On the other hand, the chase was slowly taking its toll on him. Tladi, tall, dark, and handsome, was known to have muscular legs that knew no fatigue because he could run for a long distance without stopping to rest. Endurance and stamina were among the many qualities with which he was gifted.

It was at this point that Tladi decided on another method to capture his prey. After making certain that the animal did not see him, he quietly and unobtrusively crept ahead of it; the numerous trees and bushes provided natural cover. He found a thicket and quickly laid a simple, but ingenious, trap made out of giant forest creepers.

After testing it several times, the warrior crept back to his original position. Tladi was relieved to see the handsome beast still grazing not far from where it had last been. Without wasting time, he gave chase, skillfully directing it towards the trap. The antelope got tangled in the thicket, and he was on it before it could escape; the trap could only hold it for a brief moment. Shortly thereafter, a blow to the head from a heavy knobkerrie made its knees wobble, and the creature finally collapsed to the ground. There were tiny trickles of blood coming from its nostrils as it wriggled slowly.

Tladi set about untangling the rope, wrapping it in a neat coil, and went back to where he had hidden his shield, hunting knife, and three light spears. He spotted the tree, underneath which his weapons were hidden, and made for it. Later, as he approached his trap, the antelope, which he had thought dead, disappeared into a clamp of bushes with one desperate bound.

This was unthinkable. Tladi ran after it. It was a race he was to remember long afterwards. The animal was considerably weakened and paused momentarily now and then for breath, but it still ran as fast as a man. The warrior stumbled and fell several times. Undergrowth tore his skin. He pressed on, hewing a way with his great knife when creepers like barbed wire fenced him in. He observed that each time he stopped, the animal also stopped. He thought of a trick. He stopped and pretended to go back but kept the animal under close observation. Then, he quietly struck out in another direction, creeping and crawling towards the antelope.

When he thought he was within striking distance, he could no longer see his quarry. Noiselessly, it had moved to some cool and shady undergrowth to rest. After much straining and peering, Tladi saw it; it was squatting and breathing heavily. He inched his way nearer and then dived towards the animal, knife first. He took care to employ the sharp edge of his knife.

After catching his breath, he dragged the animal away from the scene and sat on a rock. He was very far from home. He thought of carrying the animal on his shoulders but knew he had to regain his strength. The hunt had weakened him. Or, he could slice huge chunks and carry them in a sack and leave the rest to scavenging animals.

Later, Tladi decided to make camp and rest overnight. After building a makeshift hut, he hung the animal from overhead branches, allowing the blood to drip from its severed neck. While doing all this, his mind went back to the time, seasons earlier, when he was struck by Makopela's spear.

What baffled him the most about that time was that he remembered the day clearly when he was attacked and the life he lived soon thereafter. He remembered how people ran away from him because of his grotesque features, which led to the day he confided in his one true love, Lindiwe the village beauty, about his plan of seeking the help of a sorcerer named Zebe.

Tladi still saw himself travelling that long, dreadful journey at dead of night, towards the then forbidden land—crossing valleys and canyons and at last reaching the mountains at which Zebe the sorcerer was said to have dwelt. The most he could recall was his appeal to Zebe, who had formally announced himself as the sorcerer of Good. From thereon, he could not remember a thing, no knowledge, whatsoever, that Zebe had in fact, transformed him to Kahuru, the half-man half-leopard—the master of all men and beast.

What he did remember, though, is being reunited with his long-lost love, Lindiwe. He recalled the moment vividly because when he first laid eyes on her, he felt as if he had just awoken from the grip of a long sleep. When he asked what had happened to him, the king told him that the Oracle had put him in a deep sleep that had lasted four seasons—the length of time it took for the Oracle to restore his features to exactly what they had been before he was attacked.

And that was also the explanation that was given to the Bakhudung nation. Only a handful of people knew the link between Tladi and the leopard man. That link became a great village secret. From thereon, Tladi resumed his normal life. He was still leader of his regiment. He was also granted permission to take on a bride since it was peacetime, but the warrior opted, instead, to continue his full-fledged duty of warrior and hunter. This decision did not sit well with Lindiwe, of course, but she lived with the hope that one day he might change his mind; only time would tell.

That night, Tladi feasted on grilled liver and fillets before falling into a deep sleep. He did not sleep long before his sharp ears and acute sixth sense picked up what sounded like human footsteps approaching the camp. Instinctively, he grabbed his weapons and crawled out of the makeshift hut. He was not afraid, but he did not want to be taken by surprise. Surprise could beat the mightiest as he, himself, had experienced once in his life.

He quickly hid among the trees while keeping the camp under his watchful eye. There was a fire burning in front of the hut, so he could see whoever approached. For a long time, nothing happened. He was about to dismiss the thought as a figment of his imagination when four figures detached themselves from the dark surroundings of the forest. *Four!* He thought as he lay still, figuring how he was going to take on all the intruders without getting hurt or even killed in the process.

Whispering among themselves, the four figures approached cautiously, not because they expected an ambush, but because of the overwhelming effect of the ancient forest.

"Tladi," one of the figures called.

Tladi tensed but quickly relaxed after recognizing who they were. They were men from his regiment, young men he, himself, had trained. He somewhat relaxed, for he guessed the men had no evil intentions.

"Tladi," the young man called again, this time a little louder.

"Who goes there?" the warrior demanded, still crouched at his hiding place, his shield and spear well poised. He was not leaving anything to chance. The four young men whirled instinctively towards the voice that had come from a completely unexpected angle. They were impressed.

"It's us, great warrior, Fasimba, Mbiya, Tukolo, and Pemba." The men identified themselves. Since his eyes had grown accustomed to the darkness, the glow from the fire helped him discern their features clearly.

"Lower your weapons and tell me exactly what it is that you seek." Tladi's voice came from yet another totally unexpected direction, which meant he had swiftly and quietly moved to another position, making him a more elusive and lethal target; that is, if the young men's intention was to harm him.

"We have a message from the king," Fasimba spoke. He was the youngest of the four, six seasons Tladi's junior, which meant he was about seventeen. Like the rest of the youth his age, he admired and looked up to Tladi. He understood that Tladi had been given the title of Great, and like many other youths, he hero worshipped the young warrior and tried, in many ways, to emulate him.

"And what would that message be?"

The men whirled one more time, their mouths agape. The tall, handsome warrior was standing with his hands akimbo in front of the makeshift hut he had built. Somehow, he had managed to crawl from where he was last heard and sneak up behind them without making a sound. This was amazing; only spirits moved that way. It took a while before any of them could say a word. They were still shocked by what they had just witnessed. This, indeed, was a remarkable man, if not unusual.

"The king would like to have a word with you, great warrior. It seems as if there is some kind of emergency." Tukolo spoke this time. His eyes were still wide with amazement. He was short with muscular limbs. Evidently, the best men had been handpicked for this search party.

"Why? What has happened; does it have to do with Lindiwe or my father?" he asked as he took a step closer with raised eye brows, the only reaction he showed.

"No, great warrior. The king would not tell us, but as far as we know, Lindiwe and your father are fine and in good health." Mbiya spoke this time, a brave young warrior who was also known for his great tracking abilities.

"I wonder what could possibly be amiss," Tladi said as he stroked his goatee.

"My guess is that there might be trouble brewing up north because Mapoulo was sent with part of the Buffalo regiment to the land of the Barolong.

They (the Barolong) are the source of the distress call," it was Pemba this time, shrewd and intuitive.

"The Buffalo regiment?"

"Yes, great warrior," Fasimba concurred.

"Tukolo and Mbiya, bring down that antelope. We are leaving now."

"But, great warrior, we thought it would be easier if we rested and began in…"

"Now," Tladi's sharp voice, which cracked like a whip, startled them into compliance. Within a short while, they were walking along the path leading to the village, which at that time (dead of night) looked like a long tunnel amidst the woods.

Even with the weight of the dead antelope resting on his shoulders, Tladi set a killing pace, making the rest of the warriors jog trot at times just to keep up with him. He allowed them to rest for a little while, only at dawn, to quench their thirst when they came upon a creek.. It was only late in the second night when he decided to make camp and let his men rest overnight.

Since they were now in an open veld, Tladi could guess their current position by looking at the stars. If they resumed their journey just before daybreak, they would reach the village by noon. With this thought in mind, Tladi ordered his men to make a fire and roast some of the meat from the kill. After supper, the five warriors lay on their goatskin mats and were soon fast asleep.

Fasimba was the first to wake up, moments before the streaks of light from the horizon announced daybreak. He sat up on his mat and rubbed his eyes. He looked around and rubbed his eyes again. His heart began pounding rapidly. Tladi was nowhere to be seen. He immediately sprang to his feet and woke his colleagues.

"Tukolo, Mbiya, Pemba, wake up, men of the Bakhudung," there was a sense of urgency in his voice.

"What is the matter?" Mbiya asked; like the rest, he became fully awake.

"Where is Tladi?" was the answering question.

"What do you mean?"

"Look," Fasimba pointed at the spot where Tladi had lain to sleep the previous night. Instinctively, all the three men glanced at the empty spot.

"Perhaps he went to relieve himself," Pemba said.

"Why then, would he leave his weapons behind?"

At once, the men noticed the abandoned spears, shield, hunting knife, and knobkerrie laying among the grass right next to the mat.

"A warrior should never leave his weapons behind. He taught us that, himself," Fasimba added.

Tukolo immediately went and felt the mat with the back of his palm.

"It is cold," he said, in essence, meaning that Tladi had been gone for some time.

"But where could he be?" Fasimba was becoming alarmed. "You don't think a hyena dragged him away in his sleep, do you?" he added as an afterthought. Hyenas were known to snatch people in their sleep and carry them off into the night with their powerful jaws, especially children, who were a much more welcomed burden than adults.

At this suggestion, Mbiya laughed outright.

"I don't think this is a laughing matter at all, Mbiya," Tukolo said in slight exasperation.

"Really? I think you men forgot something. We are talking about one of the finest and toughest warriors the Bakhudung have known. No hyena could come and drag him away like he was *Makhulu* Jobe."

Makhulu Jobe was the oldest woman in the village. The rest of the men thought of how she trembled at every step and they, too, laughed but quickly restrained themselves. It was hardly the time for a joke.

For a long time, they waited on their missing commander, hoping with every moment that passed that he would reappear just as dramatically as he had disappeared. That warrior, Tladi, was very capable of doing such, but towards midday, their hopes turned to despair.

"Men of the Bakhudung," Mbiya spoke up. "We were sent on an urgent meeting to find Tladi; that we did, and I believe if we try again, we will find him once more."

Mbiya was a master trekker, and with that kind of conviction in his tone, the rest of the men knew he was not likely to give up. Therefore, they all agreed to search for their missing comrade.

"What will we tell the king if we come back empty handed?" Fasimba had asked earlier on, and no one could give an answer.

After a quick meal, the warriors began their search. What was most amazing was that there were no footprints to follow or any other clues such as broken twigs or flattened grass to point out as to which direction Tladi had headed. Nonetheless, they continued the search, calling out his name at times when they were either in the thickest part of the forest or an open plain, with canyons ahead and below.

It was nightfall when the search party decided to rest. Morale was at an ultimate low. The hard, cold fact was that Tladi was missing and not likely to be found. They ate their supper in silence, each wondering what the next step to take would be.

"What if Tladi decided to wake while we were asleep and head on to the village without us?" Pemba asked, amidst a mouthful of roasted meat and boiled millet.

It took a while for the question to sink in. This was a possibility none had thought about until now.

"Yes, that's true," Fasimba said thoughtfully.

"I wonder why that did not occur to us earlier on. I mean, Tladi is capable of doing that," Tukolo added.

"But why would he leave his weapons, though?" Mbiya asked.

"Perhaps, to show us how versatile a warrior he is. I would not be surprised if he had extra spears hidden somewhere," Mbiya suggested.

There was suddenly a glimmer of hope. The more they talked about the possibility of this maneuver taken by their missing commander, the stronger they believed that Tladi had headed on to the village on his own. After all, the message from the king was urgent, and "the lion's roar" was law.

Without further delay, the young warriors were homeward bound, traveling all night until they reached the village early the next morning, just after the first crow. Despite their fatigue, they headed straight to the royal compound, where they found the king and his council anxiously awaiting their arrival.

There was tension in the hut that kept building every moment as the young warriors knelt and bowed cordially before the king.

"I see you, young men, but who I don't see is the son of Ndaba, the poet and orator. Your orders were not to come back until you found him and brought him forth."

The king's voice broke the silence. On the other side of the fire, the young men quickly raised their heads and faced the king—completely dumbfounded.

Since Mbiya was the oldest among them, only he would be the designated speaker before the king. He nervously cleared his throat.

"It is, also, to our great surprise that the great warrior known as Tladi is not here with you."

"What is it that you are talking about, young man?" the king asked.

"We were expecting to find Tladi here," Mbiya replied.

"And just how is that possible, young man? All four of you were assigned with the task of finding Tladi and bringing him here after delivering the king's urgent message," It was Monaheng, the king's advisor, who spoke this time.

"Yes, O great one. We found Tladi and delivered the message that the king seeks his audience and soon."

"So now *where* is he?"

"We thought he was here," Mbiya answered, wiping his sweaty brow with his palm. He was almost convinced that the king and his council were putting on an act.

"What insolence is this?" Swathi fumed with exasperation.

"May I be allowed to speak, O great king?" Fasimba raised his right hand unconsciously.

"Speak up, son of Motelebane," the king said.

Fasimba gave a vivid description of their entire mission and ended up by saying,

"The amazing thing is that there were no physical leads pointing to which direction he headed, not even a single footprint. Tladi vanished like a spirit of the forest."

Swathi and the rest of the elders looked at each other in genuine shock and amazement. This was bizarre to say the least. For a long time, there was grave silence in the room. Only the early morning, village life activity could be heard—the pounding of the pestle and mortar, the sweeping of compounds, the bleating of sheep, the clucking of chickens and all other sounds that indicated that the peace loving and merry village was beginning its day.

"Young men, you are all excused. Go and rest; we will send for you when the need arises."

Following the traditional farewell offered to the king, the four young warriors rose, bowed cordially, and left in silence. Each one of them was more puzzled now than ever before.

"What do you make of this, O king?" asked Mophosho, the sub chief. He had been silent all along. He also had personal reasons for feeling disturbed about the whereabouts of Tladi. He would have to face his daughter, Lindiwe, the village beauty, and come up with a logical explanation.

"This, indeed, is strange to say the least," the king replied in deep thought.

"It is happening to us all over, again," Monaheng added.

"Especially at our moment of great need. I wonder if we have offended our gods and ancestors in anyway," it was the old man, Thulani who spoke this time.

"That cannot happen. We have never failed to appease our ancestors and the gods with sacrifices, even during times of plenty. Like we have seen for as long as I can remember," the king said.

"But then, where is Tladi? Only he has the answer to thwart this upcoming threat," the old man, Thulani, said matter-of-factly.

"No need to panic, great men. The gods and our ancestors cannot forsake us. Not now when we need them more than ever. Think people, there is no smoke without fire. There is a reason behind this young man's disappearance. We may know the reason soon, later, or maybe never. What we ought to do, now, is mobilize our entire army as quickly and as quietly as possible. We do not want to stir fear into the hearts of our people just yet. That's why we have to do this now and quick."

Swathi's power of reasoning logically, even in the face of a major crisis, was being tested to the utmost.

Everyone in the room agreed with the king. The cause of this alarm was that the regiment that had been sent to the land of the Barolong had returned the previous day or, rather, what was left of it. They had gone with Mapoulo in command to spy on the Tompiki, and the news they brought back was even more gruesome than what king Swathi and his council expected.

CHAPTER 12

MAPOULO AND HIS MEN reached the land of the Barolong just after the old moon paved way for the new, meaning they had marched for three days straight. Upon seeing the first huts, Mapoulo ordered the Buffalo regiment to halt. He did so by raising his hand, and almost instantly, the men disappeared without a sound. But, there was no immediate danger; Mapoulo merely wanted them to stop for a brief conference. He beckoned, and the fifty men reappeared, some of them from unexpected hideouts.

"We shall first send five men to the village to size up the situation. If all is well, they shall come back and let us know."

Mapoulo could see the tension on his men's faces. They were all young men, who had never really experienced warfare, and each one of them was itching to outdo the other, so it was no problem finding volunteers. Mapoulo picked five of the fastest running youth.

"Be sure to watch each other's backs out there and let us know promptly if there is any danger lurking." Mapoulo issued the final instructions before the five men nimbly vanished into the forest.

They did not have to wait long before the scouts returned. All was well at the village, but king Moabi wanted to meet with the leader of the regiment. Mapoulo and his men marched to the village arena. It was early in the morning, and their feet were wet from the morning dew. Despite the long march, the men showed no signs of distress.

The Barolong village was not different from that of the Bakhudung, though, it was considerably much smaller in size, meaning the population was just over 75,000 men, women, and children. The buffalo regiment marched straight into the arena, where King Moabi and his army awaited them. Upon reaching the middle of the arena, facing King Moabi and his men at the western end, the buffalo regiment came to a halt.

King Moabi was standing in command. He was not physically intimidating, short with a portly belly, but he was feared for his resiliency and never-say-die attitude. The gray hair on the sides of his head indicated that he had reached middle age.

"Mapoulo, son of great warriors of the great nation known as the Bakhudung, I see the mighty Swathi, your king, was quick to respond to my cry. For that, may the ancestors grant him long life, strength, wisdom, and prosperity," King Moabi of the Barolong hailed, much to the delight of the Bakhudung warriors, who stamped their right feet in unison amidst fierce war cries.

"Yes, it is so, great king. I am here at king Swathi's behest to find out if indeed, terror lurks not too far from our lands." Mapoulo responded with his spear and shield raised above his head.

"Let the truth be told, for it shines like the moon; but first, let us appease our ancestors and the gods, who assured the safety of your journey coming here and who will see to it that you return just as safely."

Having said that, the king ordered that a cow be brought, and following numerous incantations and rituals by the local medicine man, the beast was slaughtered as a sacrifice to appease the ancestors. Mapoulo and two of his most senior lieutenants were asked to join the king and his council under the shade of an ancient and large *Morula* tree.

Three-legged stools had been arranged in front of the king and his council, evidently for the men from the Bakhudung. Although it was still morning, the rays from the sun were scourging, so Mapoulo and his men welcomed the cool shade the overhead branches provided. Back at the arena, the warriors from both villages faced each other in silence. Fifteen men had been assigned the task of skinning the cow and slicing its carcass into huge chunks that were then roasted by the women. Before long, the aroma from the roasted beef was so welcoming that after a while, warriors from both sides started talking excitedly to one another, commenting on the impending feast.

Back under the ancient Morula tree, king Moabi began by saying:

"Let me reiterate how glad I am that your gracious king responded so quickly to our plea."

"We will let him know, great king," Mapoulo assured.

"Very well," Moabi said, following a brief pause to sip *ichwala* (syrupy beer) from a gourd. The king continued after wiping the sides of his mouth. "Close to one moon ago, one of our men ventured east beyond our border on a hunting expedition, when suddenly, he saw a great cloud of dust at the north eastern horizon. According to him, this was a sight that could only be caused by many people on a hard march. Men with "big feet" as he put it. Following further investigation from a safe spot, it turns out that these people were, in fact, the Tompiki. Moabi paused and studied the faces of his audience, whose stone-cold faces showed no reaction. Obviously, the king was not telling them anything new.

"I then sent out ten of my best spies to confirm the man's story. They came back a few days later, and yes, what my man had seen was not a figment of his imagination. It was, indeed, the race of giants who we thought were a product of myth from time immemorial until now," Moabi continued.

"Then what happened?"

"That's when I sent a distress call to your king. We are obviously in the path of these people," the king replied.

"If that was for certain, then they would have attacked your village by now," Mapoulo reasoned.

"That, my son, is exactly what we thought. Shortly after I sent those messengers to alert your king, I dispatched yet another group of spies to observe these invaders. They came back with the news that the Tompiki had temporarily settled at the valley overlooked by the great *Lungile* escarpment, some two days walk from here."

Moabi stopped speaking, but he watched the Bakhudung warrior seated in front of him with ill-concealed glee, anticipating his next question. It almost annoyed Mapoulo that he should ask it, for it sounded naïve even to his own ears.

"But why would they do that?"

"Because they are obviously preparing for a major invasion not only of our village but also to our entire existence, the great Bakhudung included."

The last statement drew the wind out of Mapoulo's lungs. A long silence followed. Nothing was heard but the cluck, cluck, and cluck of a hen feeding her brood of chickens hard by. In his mind, Mapoulo was upset at king Swathi for sending him on this mission. This was way above him, he thought. Perhaps a few elders from the braves would have been most ideal, but he quickly dismissed the thought. Obviously, King Swathi had shown great confidence in him, perhaps grooming him to one day be a Great, himself.

Audibly, he quietly asked, fearing the answer,

"How many are they, great king?"

For an answer, Moabi looked above at the branches for a while and pointed. Everyone followed the direction at which his finger pointed.

"Do you see the number of leaves this tree has, my son?"

"Yes, great one."

"That's about how many they are."

This time, Mapoulo and his two lieutenants whistled in disbelief, but they quickly composed themselves.

"Great king," Mapoulo spoke up. "It will only be better if I see these men, myself, so I can give our king firsthand account. Of course, I will have to observe them from a distance. As we all know, it is not wise to stir a hornet's nest, when there is no smoke to repel them."

"That is true, my son. And in anticipation to your request, we have already assembled a junior regiment that will act as guides."

"For that I thank you, O king, on behalf of the great Swathi."

"Very well, my son. When do you wish to dispatch?" Moabi asked.

"The sooner, the better. What about tomorrow evening? I am certain that the cover of darkness will work to our advantage"

"Yes, that is true, and I have faith in your warriors. Word is that the buffalo regiment has invisible footprints, as well as being tough and resilient like the animals which they are named after."

Mapoulo smiled at the compliment, and so did his other colleagues.

"The men I brought are not even a fraction of our entire regiment because we stand 3,000 strong," the warrior boasted.

"Yes, we will need all of their strength and that of other great warriors in the whole clan. Speaking of great warriors," the king changed the subject, "How is Tladi, the son of Ndaba, the poet and orator?"

"He is fine and in good health, great king. He is always alone and hunting when not engaged in military and state affairs."

"Yes, we are forever hearing about the never-ending great deeds of that remarkable young man. The ancestors and the gods should forever be praised for restoring his features back to normal, even though it took a very long time for that to happen."

Who would ever forget?

"Yes, that is true, great king. The powers that be can never be thanked enough."

Mapoulo and his men had already stood up after bowing to the king and his council, getting set to prepare for the second phase of their mission.

"The ancestors, the gods, and the force of Good will ensure your safety," hailed one old man, who was seated beside the king. Prior to that, King Moabi's entire council was noticeably silent.

The next nightfall found Mapoulo and his men, accompanied by the Barolong escorts, headed northwards toward the *Lungile* escarpment, which overlooked the great valley where the Tompiki were last seen. It was going to be a long journey. Apart from arming themselves to the teeth, every warrior carried enough provisions to last throughout the entire mission.

The one hundred men walked in silence. Only the sound of the night, which has come to be very symbolic of Africa, was heard. This sound included the ambivalent insect world, nocturnal birds, and other animals such as hyenas and lions. It was only after the moon had set that Mapoulo ordered his men to stop and rest.

The men divided themselves into groups of twenty and spread out within an area of 100 square feet. Only small fires were to be made at each camp, with one man assigned to be sentry. Mapoulo, like the rest of his men, did not expect danger, just yet, but these were well-trained warriors, who were indoctrinated in the code of expecting the unexpected.

However, despite all these precautions, the warriors woke up to find three of their colleagues, who had camped furthest from the group, murdered. Their bellies had been disemboweled by a sharp spear. Upon witnessing this grim discovery, one of the Barolong warriors ran to Mapoulo's camp. He found Mapoulo, like the rest, folding his goatskin mat and preparing for the final phase of their journey.

"Mapoulo ... everybody, come and see—quickly!" the Barolong warrior screamed. He was gasping for breath, and his eyes were wide open.

"What happened?" Mapoulo and a few other warriors asked at the same time. They had begun racing towards the scene before the man could answer.

Mapoulo's breath whistled in his throat as he saw the bodies—deep, gaping wounds from their bellies, blood soaked all over the ground where they lay, their wide open, glazing eyes sightlessly staring at the bright morning sky.

Two of the victims were from the Barolong unit. The third, and also a sentry, was one of Mapoulo's own. The surviving warriors circled the corpses like a predator does to its intended prey before rushing in for the kill. From their faces, Mapoulo could tell that his men were just as puzzled as he was—beyond words.

"Muata of the swamps and the sky," Mapoulo exclaimed, as many thoughts flashed through his mind like meteorites.

At their current position, they were at least a day and a half away from where the Tompiki, their obvious main threat, were last seen, so this could not have been their handiwork. Besides, why would they just kill three men and spare the rest, who had virtually been at their mercy? And how could his men sleep through this onslaught without hearing a thing? These were trained warriors.

"Who could have done this?" Mapoulo asked, still staring at the bodies. For an answer, one of the warriors said:

"Look at this, Mapoulo." The man was holding a tortoise shell that contained some strange looking herbs, which produced a sickly, sweet smell. Everybody instantly recognized it. It was the rare and mysterious poison whose smell brought sleep.

"Now, why would somebody do that? Besides, our mission is supposedly secret; nobody knows we are here," Mapoulo said in disbelief. Like some of his lieutenants, he was beginning to suspect foul play on the part of the Barolong warriors, who might seek a need to frustrate this mission.

"The food we brought along has been stolen," a warrior from the Barolong unit pointed out.

"What?"

This was more bizarre than anyone imagined.

"What you are saying is that someone did all this just to steal food?" one of Mapoulo's lieutenants asked; he was perplexed to say the least. His name was Sibi.

"That is what I am telling you. There have been similar cases such as this in our land. Many hunters can bear testimony to that," said a warrior named Phoka from the Barolong unit.

"What exactly do you mean by there have been similar cases such as this one?" Mapoulo asked.

"You don't know, great warrior?" There seemed to be more questions than there were answers.

"Please enlighten us," Sibi fumed.

"Less than three seasons ago, hunters from our village would go out to hunt in the surrounding forest like we always have for countless generations. Some of these hunters would not return home but, instead, be found dead. No one knew why, but word quickly spread around the village that the forests surrounding our village were cursed with evil spirits or "killers of the night." For a while, our king sent envoys and warriors to neighboring villages to investigate the cause of this problem. As it turns out, the cause was in the form of four young men who happen to be brothers, the same brothers who were banished from your village seasons ago. They are known as "the vulture brothers."

"No one knows their hideout and mode of operation except for the fact that they are swift, cunning, and ruthless. They strike, and within a blink of an eye, they are gone. Darkness makes them bold, and darkness makes them aggressive." By now, the Barolong warrior was surrounded by men who were staring at him incredulously as they listened to this weird tale with their mouths agape.

"But men from your village still hunt. Otherwise, we would not be heading on this mission now, would we?" Mapoulo asked, suddenly engulfed by a sickening feeling, which he associated with fear, a fear he knew he had to overcome, otherwise, their mission was doomed. It was not only about the giants, anymore. They were faced with a fresh, new breed of terror that killed by the night and ever so effectively during one's sleep.

"Of course, every man who is a man, will go about his business in the forest, vulture brothers or not," was Phoka's answer.

Realizing how precarious their situation was, Mapoulo started thinking fast. This problem needed to be resolved and soon. The assailants were applying psychological warfare, something that could prove detrimental to his men's morale and a situation he did not want to be in, not when they were faced with a far more dangerous task ahead.

"This is what we will do, great men. I will need several fast, running men to go back to the village and report this matter to king Moabi. Also, we will need an antidote for this sleeping poison," Mapoulo said after much thought.

There was a murmur among the warriors as they debated among themselves if this was a good idea or not. In the end, four men were sent back to the Barolong village. Those men were never heard of again.

The second night was similar to the previous one. Mapoulo ordered his men to stop and make camp. This time, he did not divide them into smaller groups but instead, assigned more men to stand guard. As further precaution, the sentries were ordered to conduct their lookout, perched on the highest branches of surrounding trees while the rest of the warriors fell into a light sleep. The night passed with no incident.

The next morning, the warriors woke up very refreshed. Before resuming their journey, Mapoulo held a brief conference with his men. They were almost within enemy territory, so caution was their shield. He further reminded them that their mission was simply to observe and analyze, similar to the previous parties, but this time, they were to observe the Tompiki much more closely and without being detected, of course. Conflict was to be avoided at all costs if possible.

The rest of the men listened with pounding hearts. For most of them, this was to be the first taste of real war. Although confrontation was to be avoided, something could easily go wrong (as it did in such situations), and they would have to defend themselves.

It was just before noon when the *Lungile* escarpment came into sight. It was in the distance, where the thick forest broke open into a wide veld that led to numerous canyons and mountains. It was a sight of stunning beauty under a clear, blue sky.

While in the forest, Mapoulo divided his army into three groups. The first two were ordered to hide diagonally opposite each other amidst the trees. The third, mostly warriors from the renowned buffalo regiment and smaller in size with Mapoulo as leader, advanced cautiously toward the escarpment. Mapoulo would have loved to have conducted this exploit at night, but he had to observe the enemy clearly.

When they reached the open veld, he ordered his men to spread out even more as they darted hither and thither, from one thicket to the next. Spears and shields were well poised as they reached the escarpment at last and lay flat on their bellies, observing the sight below.

The thirty-five warriors, including Mapoulo, gasped in fear at what they saw: thousands of men, big and tall. They had built makeshift huts, and smoke was everywhere from the hundreds of fires that were used to prepare the afternoon meal.

They were fierce-looking men. Their bare torsos and sinewy arms were covered with red and white ochre. Many of them were armed with long machetes, and bows hung on their shoulders, with quivers full of arrows fastened to their backs. There were women and children, too, who were darting from here to there, handing the men chunks of roasted meat and pounded millet to eat.

Mapoulo and his men observed that the bulk of the men, over three thousand of them, were assembled in front of one man: most certainly their leader. He was talking to them in fierce tones, gesticulating with his arms. It was obvious to the men observing from above that these men were getting ready for something—most probably an invasion.

Although Mapoulo could not hear them clearly, he observed that they spoke in a language alien to his people and all others in the region. Their features were not of this world. He gazed far beyond the sight below, quickly noticed other traces of smoke ahead, and knew right there and then that there were more of these men in that region. They had divided themselves. He heard King Moabi's voice once more,

"Do you see the number of leaves this tree has, my son? That's about how many they are."

King Moabi's words had assumed a frightening reality. The sight below bore testimony to that. Upon seeing the women and children, he strongly believed that these people had come to take over their land and make slaves of them as he heard they did to nations they vanquished; inwardly, the warrior wept for his people.

He was about to beckon his men when a terrifying war cry reverberated on both sides of them and echoed in the valley below. Instinctively, the warriors sprang to their feet. Closing in from both sides were warriors from the Tompiki. They had their bows fitted with arrows and menacingly extended, aiming them at Mapoulo and his men. They bore their teeth in horrible grins.

Before Mapoulo could shout the order at his men to take cover by falling flat on their bellies, a volley of arrows flew at them. Several men were mortally hit. A warrior in front of Mapoulo was struck in the neck. The arrow protruded out the other side as blood sprang from the wound. The man staggered backwards and lost his footing before tumbling from the escarpment, free-falling through at least fifty feet of air and hitting the boulders down below.

The rest, who were not struck, hit the ground with their bellies before quickly standing up and answering with a volley from their own arsenal— the deadly throwing of assegais. Few of the Tompiki fell to the earth, and the rest were reloading when Mapoulo and his men began running towards the forest.

The Tompiki warriors released another volley of arrows at the retreating figures. This time, five men fell down dead, and Mapoulo felt a sharp, numb, and sickening pain on his side. He looked down to see an arrow sticking out on the side of his lower abdomen. Apparently, it had not struck him deep enough, for he was still able to run and breathe without any difficulty. The assailants gave chase.

"Shields behind your backs!" Mapoulo shouted, still unshaken by the fact that he was hit. No sooner had he said that when an arrow wheezed past his right ear and grazed the shoulder of the warrior directly in front of him. Then, Mapoulo ran like never before, and so did the rest of his men. He had chosen the fastest runners. *If only they could reach the trees!* Mapoulo thought.

At that moment, their pursuers paused to hang the bows on their shoulders and unsheathe their machetes. This pause gave Mapoulo and his men the much needed break to gain distance from their enemies, but the Tompiki ran like the wind and were quickly closing in on them by the time they reached the trees. One of the warriors from the Barolong unit was caught and mowed down.

Once in the forest, Mapoulo raised a peculiar hoop and a shower of spears met their pursuers, bringing down many. The Tompiki were stunned. They briefly paused, looked this way and that way, and resumed their chase. Mapoulo gave yet another shout and another volley of spears claimed more lives of their pursuers. This time, the Tompiki stopped and took several steps backwards, realizing for the first time that Mapoulo had lured them into a deadly ambush.

A few diehards wanted to keep up the chase, but someone stopped them. He was their leader.

"Let them go," he said panting. All men stood over six feet five inches and were very dark with wide-spread teeth.

"I say we go after them," one man insisted.

"I said no. Obviously, those men were ready for us. They led us into a nice, little trap, and as a result, we have suffered more than twice their casualties. Who knows what they have in store for us should we decide to follow? I think we underestimated these locals and paid the price. What we have to do is report this matter to the chief as soon as possible. Perhaps this will hasten his decision concerning an all-out invasion."

The rest of the men agreed with their leader. After burying their dead comrades, they negotiated the tricky terrains that led to the temporary settlement down below. These were scouts who were sent to scour the land in an attempt to know more about this unfamiliar territory. They were on their way back to the settlement when they accidentally ran into Mapoulo and his men.

Meanwhile, Mapoulo and his warriors regrouped, and jog trotted most of the journey back home. They cut their time by half as they made it a point to just rest for a little while then keep moving. Of the one hundred men sent to spy on the Tompiki, fifty-seven survived.

Upon reaching the Barolong, he did not beat around the bush, in spite of his wounds, but told King Moabi to prepare for a long and agonizing war. That was the same message he gave to king Swathi two days later before he finally collapsed. He was immediately rushed to the medicine man's compound to treat the gaping wound on his side.

Thus, when the four young men sent to find Tladi came back empty-handed, the king and his council had justified cause for alarm. The village needed

Tladi because with him, came the immortal known as Kahuru, the human leopard.

And alas! Mapoulo was never to recover from his wound. He died a few days later and was buried with full rites by a mourning village. In death, he was given the title of Great.

CHAPTER 13

THERE WERE SO MANY PEOPLE in the royal hut that evening that at times, the king would be forced to shout amidst the din in an attempt to restore order. He was holding a very serious meeting with his council of elders. Also present, were chiefs from nearby villages including Moabi of the Barolong and Morobe of the Bafokeng, a man few would forget. He had been among those at the forefront in the war against the outcasts.

The Tompiki were on the warpath. That was the cause of this emergency meeting. The first victims would most certainly be the Barolong, as they were directly in the path of these giants. Already, refugees from the Barolong and other small villages were beginning to trickle under the warm blanket of protection from the Bakhudung village, a sight that had become all too familiar during the previous war.

The main subject of the gathering was simple— the upcoming war with the Tompiki. There was one vexing problem, though. These men possessed fighting methods that were foreign to the locals. Before his untimely death, Mapoulo, on his sick bed, had described in great detail, the mechanism of the Tompiki's most lethal weapons, the bow and arrow backed by a long machete.

The power and accuracy of this strange weapon, the bow and arrow, was a force to be reckoned with because all the Bantu-speaking people in Southern Africa used the throwing spear as their primary weapon. The throwing spear's level of damage and accuracy really depended on an individual's strength. This was not the case with the bow and arrow. Its missile covered a much longer distance and with more accuracy according to the fallen warrior's report. Only Kahuru's magic spear was vastly superior (guns and cannons were not known at that time). There were many others who backed that observation, and they were the survivors of the most recent encounter with the Tompiki.

This piece of information, though vital, greatly distressed not only king Swathi, but also all the other kings in the region. Adding to that distress was the fact that the number of the Tompiki was staggering. The main question, now, was how were they going to withstand the attack when it came?

No one seemed to have an answer. Someone suggested that an envoy be sent to negotiate for peace. Many agreed with this suggestion, but it presented one major problem. Nobody could speak or understand the Tompiki language;

therefore, there would definitely be a communication problem. Although war with the Tompiki was best to be avoided, king Swathi pointed out that this was an invasion. The Tompiki were set to drive them out of their fatherland and even enslave them, as earlier events had proved. They had no choice but to face this upcoming threat head on. Even if they were to lose, they would die fighting for what belonged to them and their future generations.

Nobody could argue with that kind of reasoning. There was nothing else to do but to fight for their land and for their right to live in peace and prosperity. It was in the very early hours of the morning when the gathering dispersed. The meeting was to be resumed just before noon. It would be time to discuss strategies and maneuvers to counter this imminent attack.

The king was left alone in the massive hut to ponder the fate of his people. The fire in the middle of the room was reduced to glowing logs that gave the silent hut an eerie feeling. There was only one thought in Swathi's mind. *Where* on earth was Tladi, the son of Ndaba, the poet and orator and with him, the mighty Kahuru? With him on his side, he would fear nothing under the sun.

Also, on his mind, was the disturbing news of the four lads he banished from the village, who had turned into killers of the night, known also as "the vulture brothers." The youth had been long forgotten. It was almost taboo for young children to even utter their names, but here they had emerged into murdering scavengers who killed by the night. Bad times had, once again, come to haunt the Bakhudung.

Suddenly, the tranquility was disturbed by a vicious snarl.

"Leopard," Swathi muttered to himself.

It was the dead of night. What would a leopard be doing in the middle of a densely populated village? He was thinking about what to do next when the door opened quietly as if by a spirit. The tiny hairs at the back of his neck stood as his body tensed. His right arm slowly reached out for a weapon. Then in came Kahuru, the leopard man, the master of men and beast; Swathi's heart gave a wild, painful leap.

Tladi was not certain how long he had been asleep, but it was not long before he woke up with a start. But all was quiet, save for the snores coming from the four youths who had been sent to call him. He did not know why or what had woken him, but moments later, a soft breeze swayed the grass and trees surrounding them

"Tladi," a voice called softly from within the long elephant grass.

His heart started pounding wildly. It was a voice he had not heard in ages. It was a voice of the gods. It was a voice from the spirit world. It was the voice of Zebe, the Oracle of Good, also known as the divine sorcerer.

The warrior stood up slowly and faced the east, where the voice came from amidst the breeze. Tladi raised his arms and closed his eyes as the wind blew under his armpits.

"It is I, great Oracle," Tladi answered the strange call in a voice hardly recognizable as his own.

"My son, you are to come to me now. It is the will of the gods and the power of the forces of Good that say so," the voice was ghastly. Only few men on this earth could behold it, and that Bakhudung warrior was one of them.

"Yes, great Oracle, but my king has sent a distress call. He seeks my audience."

"You must come to me, and that time now, son of Ndaba the poet and orator," the voice insisted. It was starting to fade in the distance.

After a while, it was all quiet as if nothing had happened. He looked at the dark sky. There were patches of stars here and there as they broke through the clouds. Tladi gazed at them for a while and guessed correctly that dawn was a long way off. The warrior pondered his situation once more. Zebe, the oracle of Good, had just summoned him, and there was also that distress call from king Swathi. There was no doubt which of the two was the most important. But then, how does he explain this situation to the young men who were sent to escort him back to the village?

As an afterthought, the warrior figured it would be best to leave them sleeping and rush to see what Zebe had in store for him. The oracle lived beyond the thick forests that bounded the Bakhudung, across the plains and canyons at the great mountainous region. He lived alone in the caves. From Tladi's present position, he could almost discern the dark mountains in the east.

Without any further delay, the warrior jog trotted eastwards like a man possessed. Even though he left his spears and shield behind, he knew he was adequately protected when he was called by the Oracle, himself

Tladi kept such a steady pace that soon enough, his muscular torso was flushed with sweat. He kept running, sometimes leaping over small shrubs and avoiding numerous holes, which would have twisted an ankle and hence, hamper his rhythm. He was way beyond fatigue when he, at last, arrived at the mountains of the Oracle, just as the morning star crept from the eastern horizon.

He paused for a moment before negotiating his way to the dark caves above. It had been seasons since he was last here, and Tladi did not know what to expect this time around. The place still looked and felt the same, scary and quiet with dark caves that looked like they would devour him in one snap.

That was when it came suddenly, without warning, a crimson ball of fire that flew from one of the dark caves above and landed just a few inches from his feet. Tladi immediately knelt on one knee and covered his face with his right hand.

"I am glad you responded quickly, once again, to my call, son of Ndaba."

The voice of Zebe sounded from above, followed thereafter by a terrifying echo.

"Yes, great Oracle," Tladi said as he peaked through his fingers at the dark silhouette of the Oracle.

Although it was dark, Tladi recognized this strange man. He was a midget with shaggy gray hair that touched his shoulders and eyes that had no pupils. His long beard was twinned with strange-looking leaves. And of course, numerous bones and cowries dangled around his neck. Zebe carried no weapon, and he had no need to because he was protected by forces well beyond imagination.

"The spirit of Kahuru, the human leopard, has got to be revived," The oracle said.

Tladi looked up and was about to say something, but his great respect for this strange man refrained him. He began trembling all over.

"The ancestors and the gods, of whom I act as mediator between them and you people, have foreseen the coming of what could be a great catastrophe known to all mankind in this region of the world."

The Oracle went on to talk at great length about the Tompiki and why he thought it might take more than Kahuru and the unified army to repel this invasion.

"As master of all men and beast," the Oracle continued, "You will have to exercise your utmost will to utilize the power from which you partly come, the power of the mighty cat family." At that moment, five fully-grown leopards crept from the dark caves and partially surrounded the warrior before sitting on their hind legs. Upon sensing them, Tladi slowly looked up at the Oracle. He had vanished. Only his voice was audible.

"On his second coming, Kahuru will be ten times mightier than he was before." At that moment, lightning flashed everywhere as a strong wind uprooted shrubs and pelted Tladi with tiny particles of dust and stones. The sheer force of the wind swayed him this way and that way, and just as suddenly as it had begun, this phenomenon ceased.

Tladi looked up and saw a huge, silver ball of light floating towards him. He maintained his posture and let his body relax, for he was not sure what to expect. When the light covered him, a strange feeling suddenly engulfed his body. First, he smelled the leopards. His body started bulging. The bone structure in his face was moving into different places. He was changing. His ears assumed an almost triangular shape. Whiskers shot out. His tooth structure changed, too; canines and carnassials took shape. Soft, dark fur covered his face, arms, and torso. His fingers dilated, and his hands turned into paws that still maintained their human mechanism. His feet also attained a similar revolution. A tail shot out a little above his buttocks. A strange metamorphosis had taken effect. Once more, Tladi was transformed into a half-man half-leopard, an alter ego known as Kahuru, the human leopard.

The fabulous creature sprang to his feet with a vicious snarl. He was a very frightening sight, indeed. There was a shining, bronze spear on the ground with a small blowing horn and several amulets. These, Kahuru picked up immediately. The spear he recognized as the spear of Good, which would fly back to his paw when the target was met.

The dwarf Oracle looked down at him and said,

"Go now, Kahuru, and fulfill your worth on this earth."

With that, the half-man half-beast turned and hurtled down the mountain at incredible speed, that of a leopard on two feet, leaping over rocks, shrubs, and boulders with breathtaking ease. In no time, the forest swallowed him. A while later, the five leopards followed suit.

Zebe gazed at the spot where he had last seen Kahuru and wondered whether this was going to be the human leopard's last quest. A sad feeling dawned on the Oracle. If Kahuru succumbed, then the remarkable lad known as Tladi was gone forever.

"May the ancestors and the force of Good be with, you son of Ndaba," The Oracle said softly to himself. He knew that Kahuru and the Bakhudung faced a mammoth of a war, one that they likely might not win.

CHAPTER 14

"KAHURU!" SWATHI EXCLAIMED IN a hoarse whisper as he sprang to his feet.

"Greetings, great king, it has been a very long time," the human leopard said as he took a step forward.

"Oh, let the great ancestors forever be praised." The king had not yet recovered fully from his initial shock.

"Yes, here I am, great king."

For a while, Swathi gazed at the immortal standing before him without uttering a word. Kahuru looked much bigger and stronger compared to the last time the two saw one another. His eyes glowed in the semi-darkness. The muscular thighs, knotted belly, and the thick biceps and triceps, with no ounce of fat, told the king, and rightly so, that the immortal he was looking at possessed the strength of twenty of his strongest warriors put together.

"Great warrior, we are facing a grave crisis," the king said. He was much more composed this time as he rapidly recovered from his shock.

"That I know very well, but fear not, for Kahuru is here. We have a duty and a sworn pact to uphold."

This seemed too good to be true. At times, the king wondered if this was a dream from which he would wake up very soon, and discover, to his dismay, that there was no Kahuru after all. But this was happening right before his very eyes. This was no fantasy. Kahuru, the human leopard, the master of men and beast, the mightiest in the land and beyond, was standing right before him in the royal hut.

"What can I say, mighty warrior? Except that we are faced by a mighty enemy who threatens our very existence," Swathi said almost in lamentation.

On the other hand, Kahuru could not help but notice that the king's hair had turned a little grayer since the last time he had seen him, which was shortly after the war with the outcasts. Swathi had fought bravely and gallantly, symbolic of a true king, and had since won the mighty Kahuru's respect. But the human leopard knew that this time, the upcoming war would need a little more than just sheer bravery. Wit, iron discipline, proper training, great leadership, and determination were the keys to ultimate victory.

"What is the current position of the Tompiki?" Kahuru asked, showing his fangs as he spoke.

"They are advancing towards the Barolong."

"Approximately how long should it take them before they actually reach the village?" It was obvious that Kahuru had something in mind.

"Considering the fact that they are marching in one whole group, it should take them at least ten days to get to the Barolong Village" King Swathi had assigned a small regiment of warriors who spied incessantly on these invaders. They reported only to the king on a daily basis.

"When you say, "one whole group," about how many are we talking about?" The human leopard wanted to know.

"About 31,000 strong and not counting their women and children," Swathi answered.

Kahuru simply nodded as he sat on a stool on the other side of the glowing fire, still firmly holding the ultimate weapon—the spear of Good. Swathi also sat on the three-legged, royal stool, facing Kahuru.

"The Barolong should immediately evacuate their village if they wish to survive as a nation," Kahuru said at last.

"But great warrior, that's impossible. Their village will be run down and burned to the ground," Swathi protested.

"Well, nothing can prevent that from happening, now, but would you rather they burn down the village with the women and children?" Kahuru asked, knowing that the king could give only one answer

"Absolutely not," Swathi had suddenly gotten the picture because he quickly added, "That will be my first directive when my meeting with all the kings in this region, including Moabi, resumes in the morning.

"That is more like it, great king," Kahuru said as he stood up, getting ready to leave.

"Great warrior, are you not going to attend the meeting? Surely your presence will boost the much-needed morale among the villagers and us, not to mention the region as a whole," the king said as if perplexed by Kahuru's seemingly imminent departure.

"I am fully aware of that, great king, and as for my presence, let us keep that between ourselves, at least until I announce it, myself." He was already at the door of the royal hut.

"And when will that be, great warrior?"

Kahuru paused and turned around, gnashing his teeth but not menacingly and said:

"When day breaks."

"Will you still need Lindiwe, the daughter of Mophosho, to attend to your needs?"

The name, Lindiwe, froze the human leopard dead on his tracks. He paused for a long without facing the king. Swathi had hit on a sensitive nerve, and he knew it.

"Yes, if she wants to," Kahuru answered slowly before he vanished into the darkness. Not long after, a nearby cock flapped its wings majestically and crowed. Before long, other crows could be heard in unison from the far end of the sleeping village. Dawn was not too far off.

The king stretched his arms and lay on a buffalo hide. He fell into a light sleep with what looked like a faint smile on his lips. Yes, it was not a dream. The human leopard known as Kahuru had returned.

The following morning, king Swathi met as planned with his council of elders and the kings from all other regions. This time, the meeting was held in the royal compound in order to accommodate this large gathering. Swathi was seated at the western end of the compound. He was flanked, as usual, by Mophosho, the sub chief, and Monaheng, the chief advisor.

There was a cold, morning breeze, which shook the overhead branches. The morning village activity could be heard, which was mostly signified by the sound of the pestle and mortar as the women pounded the sorghum and millet. But within the royal compound, the atmosphere was tense. The meeting had been adjourned the night before without coming up with a proper strategy as to how this imminent attack from the Tompiki was to be withstood.

Time was running out, and everyman at that meeting knew that a solution had to be reached and agreed upon before sunset. For all they knew, war could break out before the next day was over, in spite of the fact that king Swathi was getting daily briefings about the movements of the enemy.

Thus, all the kings in the region who had pled allegiance to king Swathi looked at him for an answer. After making sure that everybody was present, the king stood up and cleared his throat. He was clad in full war gala, capped by the twin ostrich feathers sticking from his hair. The ostrich feathers and the crocodile teeth necklace hanging around his neck signified his kingship.

"Great kings, fine commanders of even finer warriors. I Swathi, king of the Bakhudung, welcome you once more."

His subjects stood up and acknowledged the greeting by shouting and stamping their feet in unison before seating down. The king had to wait for a while before the deafening roars ceased.

"The fact that we are here, once again, tells us that it is time for action. We have said enough, and it is time for us to put our words into practice," the king paused for a while and gazed at his audience. At that moment, his eyes lit up like a shooting star, the only emotion he showed.

"The ancestors and the gods have answered our plea. And now, I am quite certain victory will be ours."

Following this statement, there was a loud murmur of approval; although, it was pretty obvious that most of the men did not quite share the king's optimism. Something struck them as odd, though. There was absolute conviction in his tone of voice, and when he spoke, he seemed to be speaking to somebody at the back of the gathering. Morobe, king of the Bafokeng, was among the first to notice.

"All of us remember," the king continued "the war we fought against the outcasts seasons ago. We came together as one, and had on our side, and still have, one of the fierce and strongest warriors known to men."

At that moment, Morobe's heart skipped a double heartbeat. He was seated at the very front, so he quickly turned his head, giving his neck a painful jolt. He let out a scream of shock, surprise, and relief—all rolled into one. Everybody followed suit, and the reaction was predictable. Pandemonium, if not for a short while, became inevitable.

Kahuru had dramatically appeared. He was standing behind the gathering all this time. The men facing the gathering, that is if we exclude the king, were briefed so that they were to show absolutely no emotion the moment Kahuru entered the compound as they were to be the first ones to see him.

How the mighty Kahuru managed to sneak through the village undetected before appearing at that gathering is still a great mystery up to this day; there have been countless versions about that dramatic moment, many of which are best left unsaid.

"Great kings and great warriors, it is with great joy and pleasure that I present unto you Kahuru, the master of men and beast!" Swathi shouted, his booming voice adding some dramatic effect to the occasion.

The men, having quickly recovered from their shock, roared like never before. Kahuru merely stared, his face stern and cold like a rock. When he walked to the front of the gathering, his sinewy body swayed in the light morning breeze. The immortal was armed as usual with the ultimate weapon—the spear of Good.

The human leopard raised his bronze spear above his head and gnashed his canines. Many men in the audience gasped. Kahuru was, indeed, a very tough sight to behold. And when he spoke, he said, "Men of men, it is time to prepare for war. There is no time to waste."

"Umm!" His audience affirmed.

"King Moabi," the human leopard addressed the Barolong king. "It is imperative that your people vacate their village and soon."

Moabi immediately stood up. He was seated next to Morobe, king of the Bafokeng. He cleared his throat and said, "Mighty warrior, the mightiest in the land and beyond, it is with great honor that I have lived to see this day when I speak to the great warrior in person. Yes, it goes without saying that my village is in the direct path of these marauders. But needless to say, the bulk of our army stands guard as we speak to neutralize any forthcoming attack. This, I believe, will give us enough time to plan a massive counterattack."

Kahuru, who never missed a chance to advertise his increasingly rational point of view, is said to have replied the king,

"True to word, Moabi, but what you are saying is that your warriors should be the sacrificial lambs. What will happen is that, after the Tompiki are through with them, they will turn on the women and children and massacre them like flies. Thereafter, they will have captured all your grain and cattle, thus replenishing their supplies. A rejuvenated army will then face us, a position none of us will cherish."

For a while, there was dead silence among the men. Even king Swathi racked his brain for a possible solution. On the other hand, Moabi nodded his head in agreement. He realized that he could not expose his people to this grave danger. At last, he asked matter-of-factly, "What then, does the mighty Kahuru propose?"

"Let a regiment be dispatched at once to escort all the women, children, and cattle back here. They should carry as much grain as possible, and what is left behind, should be destroyed and all the wells poisoned."

There was a loud murmur amidst the gathering. Many did not understand the logic behind burning food and poisoning wells.

"Now, why should we resort to such measures, Kahuru?" It was Morobe, king of the Bafokeng, who asked this time.

"The answer is simple, great king. The Tompiki are in unfamiliar territory, so they move in a large group, which makes them slow. They hope to get their food from the villages they vanquish, so let hunger be our immediate weapon against them."

To this, the men cheered. Even Swathi stood up and applauded the human leopard by stamping his massive foot several times on the ground. Afterwards, all the men, including Kahuru, gathered even closer and spoke in low voices. It was almost noon when everybody dispersed. An entire regiment was dispatched to the Barolong village to carry out Kahuru's order. Kahuru was named commander-in-chief and was to be assisted by three war generals: Swathi, king of the Bakhudung, Morobe of the Bafokeng, and the ever-courageous Makaba of the Sotho-Tswana. The rest of the sub chiefs were issued numerous responsibilities. Mophosho, for instance, was assigned with the task of hiding the women, children, old men, grain, and cattle in various parts of the primeval forest, which up until then, were not well known to the people due to tales of myths, and dread that surrounded them.

CHAPTER 15

WHEN THE TOMPIKI ARRIVED at the Barolong
village, they were met by a ghastly silence. With
neither a soul nor animal in sight, two well-armed
regiments were the first to arrive. The rest of the
Tompiki, including their women and children, had
made camp some thirty miles away. The two
Tompiki regiments flanked the village from the
east and west. Both regiments stood 7,000 men
strong.

With extended arrows and bared machetes, the
fourteen thousand men let out a terrifying war cry
and charged at the silent village. Since they were
expecting a resistance, some warriors flanking
from the east mistook their comrades coming from
the west as the enemy and vice versa. Before
anyone could stop them, some timid warriors from
both units sent a volley of arrows at the others,
and before they realized their mistake, a total of
twenty men lay dead or seriously wounded.

Both regiments halted in the middle of the arena
as they faced each other. The sun was setting, and
the shadows were long. For a moment, the
Tompiki were stunned. Could this be a trap? With

this thought in mind, one of the leaders from the eastern regiment gesticulated by waving his machete in a circular motion, in essence, telling his men to scour the village. This they did almost by reflex action, and the warriors raided every beehive hut like ravenous, wild dogs.

They brought down huts by slashing the grass with their razor sharp machetes and pushed the surrounding fences by the sheer strength of many. It did not take long to find out that all these efforts were unnecessary. The village was completely deserted save for a chicken here and there. This was strange. The warriors reassembled at the arena.

"Where are they?" Their leader demanded. He was tall and had sinewy limbs.

"They are nowhere to be found. The village has been deserted," One warrior replied.

"Yes, I can see that, but where could they be?" The leader insisted.

"They could be anywhere," another warrior said as he waved his hand at the surrounding forest.

"And it looks like they have been gone for a while. Spread out, again, and find out where they keep their grain. Take as much as you can."

Thinking that their replenishments would come from the full granaries of the Barolong, the Tompiki had left with a day's provision, but they were amazed to discover that the granaries were absolutely bare. Not a handful of grain was obtainable anywhere, and the total absence of any kind of life, save for a few chickens, had an eerie and depressing effect.

After this discovery, the Tompiki reassembled at the village arena. Darkness was rapidly approaching, and with it, came the natural fear of the unknown. Their leader felt that it was too risky to journey back and rejoin the rest of the army located thirty miles north, so he ordered his men to camp in the arena. A large fire was made, which could be seen from far.

The wood used from the fire came from the ancient logs that surrounded the village, which was close to three miles in circumference. A strong guard was placed around the village to keep watch all through the night. The rest of the warriors rationed out whatever little food they brought among themselves. It appeared as if it was going to be a long and cold night.

At around midnight, the fire began to die down rapidly. Some men were ordered to replenish the wood. Few men were dispatched because the bulk of the Tompiki regiment had spread their mats on the ground and had fallen asleep.

Meanwhile, not too far off, Kahuru and a regiment of 2,000 men crouched among the trees of the surrounding forest and watched all these developments. All of these men knew what to do when Kahuru gave the signal. These were handpicked men from the renowned buffalo regiment.

Kahuru gave the command, which was echoed sentence by sentence to every lieutenant in the sub regiments. Kahuru led a party of 500 men towards the eastern side of the village. In uncanny silence, the men crawled and tiptoed towards the entrance. When they were about fifty yards away, the human leopard snarled like the leopard he was. This was a signal to his men, telling them to halt. The young moon had already set, so any physical gesture by hand would have been lost among the warriors barely ten feet behind.

The warriors, including Kahuru, observed that there was an armed guard of about two hundred Tompiki at the entrance. Naturally, they had concentrated most of their guard at the western side of the village, where they expected an attack to come if any, the simple reason being that the forest was thickest on that side.

As Kahuru noted, most of the Tompiki who were guarding the entrance were beginning to doze into a light sleep. The long march and the eerie silence of the recently deserted village were beginning to take its toll. Kahuru snarled, again, and the warriors spread out as much as they could without losing contact. Their spears and shields were well poised.

Some of the Tompiki did hear these snarls but mistook them as sounds of the night. When, at last, the warriors were within striking distance, which was half a spear throw away, Kahuru gave vent to a long and terrifying inhuman war hoot, and a volley of well thrown spears showered on the Tompiki. The night, at once, was filled with terrified shrieks of death as the audible sound of sharp blades embedded into soft, human flesh.

Before the Tompiki recovered, another hoot pierced the night, and another set of spears rained in on them, bringing down many of the Tompiki. By the time the remaining Tompiki managed to extend their arrows and return their own volley, their assailants had already closed in on them. Kahuru's men had anticipated this counterattack by positioning their shields accordingly. As a result, most of the arrows harmlessly bounced off their shields. Although, it's safe to note that a handful were either mortally hit or wounded.

With the human leopard in command, whose sight alone compelled many of the surviving Tompiki at the forefront to take to their heels, the warriors closed in by using their unused weapons as stabbing spears. Before long, it was all over. The very few Tompiki who had survived this onslaught ran to alert the rest of the army at the very interior of the Barolong village.

With no further delay, Kahuru instructed his men to carry as much of the fallen Tompiki's weapons as possible—their bows and arrows including the deadly machetes. Following this, the warriors turned and ran as fast as they could and were soon swallowed by the surrounding forest.

The reaction of the rest of the Tompiki was predictable, and they did exactly what Kahuru had expected them to do. An alarm was raised, and the bulk of the Tompiki warriors quickly mobilized themselves. After leaving a skeleton crew to stand guard at the village, the Tompiki decided to give chase. They were not going to let the aggressors go unpunished. This conviction was fueled more by the sight of their dead comrades, who lay dead at and around the village entrance.

The Tompiki were willing to brave the menacing forest and go after the attackers. With this willingness in mind, their leader had thrown caution to the wind. They were in unfamiliar territory; the forest ahead of them was totally unknown. Amidst war cries, their leader, with the type of courage known only to the brave, urged his men to follow him. With incredible speed, the Tompiki followed. Their leader ran like a man possessed.

No sooner had the last Tompiki vanished into the forest then the remaining of Kahuru's 1,500 men raided the village, annihilating the 500 or so Tompiki who were left to guard what had become their temporary fortress. Soon afterwards, the entire village was set ablaze, and the jovial warriors disappeared into the forest. The battle that was later to be known as "Rolong" had just begun.

Meanwhile, the chase proved to be a nightmare for the Tompiki. This part of the forest was alien to them. Darkness even made their task all the more difficult. They could hear the enemy far ahead. Kahuru and his men knew they were being chased, so instead of increasing the distance between them and their pursuers, the human leopard ordered his men to jog trot, thus sucking the enemy deeper and deeper into the forest.

They dodged trees and undergrowth with uncanny dexterity, but the same could not be said about the Tompiki, who constantly ran into barriers and not to mention many who fell victim to the deadly bush traps that had previously been set in anticipation of a chase like this one. The traps were simple and effective, especially one that was a ten by ten foot hole and six feet deep. At the bottom, were several two foot-long sticks sharpened with great thoroughness and placed with the sharp ends sticking out. The holes were then covered with flimsy branches. These pits of death claimed quite a few Tompiki lives.

Many wanted to give up the chase and return to the village, but their leader would not let them. A lot of his good men had died, and he would not let the enemy escape unscathed. What was he going to tell his chief? That almost half of his army was killed, and he did not have a single prisoner to show for it? No, he did not think so. They were going to finish this battle regardless of the consequences.

As this thought came to mind, the noise far ahead of the retreating fugitives suddenly stopped. This change made the Tompiki leader howl at his warriors to halt. It took a while for everybody to catch his breath. It was still dark, and the forest looked like one hairy monster.

"It seems as if the enemy has stopped running," the leader said panting. "We must approach with caution. They know we are coming," he added.

"Or perhaps they spread out in different directions, Bamwa," one warrior remarked.

Bamwa, their leader, considered this point for a moment. They were deep in the forest, and it was possible that they were being led into a trap. He began, for the first time, to realize the folly of his mad charge. He had reacted on emotions instead of wisdom. There was only one thing to do.

"We must return to that village at once. It is time our entire army was mobilized, so we can crush these people once and for all."

Everybody echoed this suggestion. Actually, many had not seen the logic of having gone after the enemy at that time of day in the first place. It was more like a suicide chase because they had suffered countless casualties.

The Tompiki began retracing their footsteps westwards. All of a sudden, the journey back was not an easy one. The night was filled with terrifying war cries. Once in a while, without warning, spears would shower at them from unexpected angles. What was worse was that their assailants would vanish without a trace. *If only they could reach the open veld*, Bamwa thought.

It was then that he and his men witnessed a strange occurrence, which many could not readily explain with words. As they were on the retreat, Bamwa instructed his men to spread into Indian file as much as possible. This was done so that when another attack came, they could afford to spare fewer casualties. At the head of this retreat, was a magnificent man with well-formed muscles. He seemed to be Bamwa's assistant, judging from his enthusiasm.

The Tompiki kept running in this formation for a long time. There had been no further attacks, thus far, despite the war cries that came from all directions some near some far that made it look like the number of Kahuru's men was three times more than it actually was. Meanwhile, Bamwa's assistant and a small band of warriors had increased their distance from the rest. That's when the attack came, and Bamwa and his men were treated to a sight out of the realm of reality.

First, there was an ear-splitting roar that momentarily froze Bamwa and his warriors. There seemed no doubt as to what it was, a leopard, but what disturbed the men, was that this particular roar seemed to come from a different world. The roar came from a leopard, alright, but it kind of sounded human at the same time. While never afraid of the normal, they were completely cowed by the abnormal.

And right before their eyes, a dark and monstrous figure leapt from a tree up ahead and landed on Bamwa's assistant, the impact causing him to drop his machete almost at once. The figure snarled as it grabbed the Tompiki warrior by the head, dug its claw-like hand at the man's throat, and ripped out his larynx. A gush of air was heard moments before the blood spurted out of the wound. Kahuru!

The half-man half-leopard immediately faced the stunned men and roared, once more. His eyes glowed in the dark as he showed his fangs. He then hurled his spear at the nearest warrior, which pierced his belly until it protruded from the other side. And right before the eyes of the petrified Tompiki, the spear disembodied and flew back at the owner's hand. Kahuru snarled, once more, and vanished into the darkness. This whole process lasted two double heartbeats, giving the Tompiki no time to react.

Despite the horrors of the previous raid caused by the Buffalo regiment, this sight seemed to be removed from reality. Even Bamwa, one of the Tompiki's fiercest fighters, shuddered. What had they just witnessed? A man who looked like a leopard? It simply was not possible, but yet it was true. The reactions of disgust and sickening horror were unavoidable. Kahuru and the Bakhudung had achieved the ultimate in the horror game. The Tompiki had to show that they, too, could rig up horrors hitherto undreamed of. And to achieve this objective, there was no choice but link once again with the main army that still awaited their return.

With an unflagging determination common to men at bay, the Tompiki ran like the wind, many speechless from horror at what they had just witnessed. They had to reach the open veld now more than ever. The normal military precision was lost as it now became every man for himself, and the devil take the hindermost!

It was almost dawn by the time they reached the veld only to be confronted by an incinerated village. Goaded by fatigue due to lack of sleep, hunger, and mainly thirst, the Tompiki approached the two main village wells with caution. They desperately needed to quench their thirst before undertaking the long march back to the rest of the army.

To their surprise and relief, there had been no further molestations to this point, so they quickly drew water from the wells and drank in large proportions. Thereafter, they began the long march, constantly on the alert to neutralize any surprise attacks. But none were forthcoming. What were the Bakhudung up to this time?

Bamwa did not feel comfortable at all. The same could be said about the rest of his men. They were tired and hungry and thus, very vulnerable. This vulnerability was evident by the way each warrior dragged his feet; an attack now could mean doom

They had not gone far before eight men in front of Bamwa collapsed as though pole-axed. At first, their leader thought this was due to fatigue, but after taking a closer look, he saw that these men were going through painful convulsions. They squirmed all over the ground, their faces contorted in painful expressions as they clawed at the earth with their fingernails and frothed from the mouth. They rolled this way and that way, grasping their bellies real tight.

Before long, everybody around him was dropping to the ground like ripe fruits. Some yelled and called out to the gods to save them. One man chewed at his tongue in sheer agony. It looked as if some supernatural evil had dawned on them.

"W-we have been poisoned," one warrior shouted amidst the groans.

"Poisoned?" How? What do you mean poisoned?" Bamwa asked with a sinking heart. His knees began to wobble uncontrollably, and that's when it dawned on him, *the wells*; their enemies had poisoned the wells!

"Quick, those who don't feel sick scour the surroundings, and look for old cow dung and *umtuma* fruit." Even as he said that, his vision began to blur, and his stomach growled, and sharp pains followed. As he fell to his knees, clasping his stomach with a salty sensation filling his mouth; everything began spinning. All around him, warriors were falling in droves.

As death came to Bamwa, he heard war cries coming from all angles as Kahuru's men moved in for the final onslaught. Of the fourteen thousand men sent to raid the Barolong in the first step of the Tompiki's campaign of terror, less than a tenth returned to the main army. These were men who were who were lucky enough to have escaped with their lives after the very first attack. The Bakhudung and the unified army had won the battle of Rolong, but all-out war was coming.

CHAPTER 16

A BATTALION OF 25,000 MEN assembled in the vast arena of the Bakhudung village. The full moon glared upon them. Their faces were painted with bright red ochre, giving them a sinister look. A drumbeat could be heard at regular intervals. In essence, the message was clear—it was time for all-out war, and the entire army was armed to the teeth, fully prepared to face this oncoming menace head on.

When Kahuru, Swathi, Morobe, and Makaba appeared at the southern end of the arena, the battalion stood up like one man. The human leopard stepped forward and snarled. His well-formed muscles could be discerned, even from far.

"Children of the land, the moment of full-scale war has finally come." Kahuru had to wait for the deafening roar to cease before he continued.

"We have reason to believe that the Tompiki have mobilized their entire army and are heading this way at full stride. These are men who are now bloodthirsty for revenge. They are full of fire, and thus, we have to fight fire with fire."

Following the battle of Rolong, Kahuru and his men returned to the Bakhudung village, where the news of victory was received with mammoth accolades. Kahuru's plan had worked to perfection. It was now time to get down to serious business. For all they knew, the war with the giants had not even begun.

Upon assembling the entire army, which consisted of warriors from all the nations that pled allegiance to king Swathi and recognized him as sole ruler, Kahuru decided to implement the rest of his war plan with the help of his generals. He had witnessed the Tompiki's fighting prowess and methods. They were very able fighters, tough, brave, and resilient. The element of surprise had worked in favor of Kahuru and his men thus far. The element of surprise and pure strategy, on the part of the immortal, had ensured them total victory at the battle of Rolong.

On the other hand, Kahuru knew that the unified army would lose if they opted for straight up, conventional warfare. The Tompiki had learned from their previous mistakes and were not likely to falter this time around. Although the Tompiki lost almost two regiments at Rolong, they still stood well over 25,000 strong. And when on the offensive, they could be totally ferocious, as seen by the mad charge that they made at Kahuru's regiment in the forest.

Adding to those complications, the Tompiki's primary weapon, the bow and arrow, when properly used, could prove to be a serious threat to the unified army. However, like any other great general, Kahuru decided, with the help of his assistants, to use the unified army's weaknesses as strengths. The Tompiki were not only big in size but also in number, thus very much exposed, whereas the unified armies, being smaller in size, could break into even smaller units, making it easier for them to hide and then resurface at will.

The unified army would have to fight battles that they could win, and in the process, capture weapons that they could then use against their enemies. As was the case at the battle of Rolong, the enemy would be supplying them and in the process, growing weaker as the Bakhudung and the unified army grew stronger.

After the battle of Rolong, Kahuru and his generals estimated that they had approximately two moons in which to prepare for the second phase of the war. He knew that their enemies would be better prepared this time. They had obviously underestimated the locals and were not willing to pay the same price again.

With the help of the ever courageous Makaba of the Sotho–Tswana, Kahuru handpicked a special unit to which he was to oversee its training. The regiment was comprised of young men between the ages of nineteen and twenty-two. The chosen youth had been known to be brash with no great regard for authority, but with Kahuru as their main overseer, the slightest idea of insubordination quickly vanished at the mere mention of his name.

The regiment stood 5,000 strong, and the two commanders, Kahuru and Makaba, subjected them to the most gruesome training known. They were woken up early in the morning and ordered to jog trot forty to fifty miles daily. This regiment bathed under freezing waterfalls and was, at times, ordered to kill a buffalo with their bare hands. This particular training was discontinued after a while because of inevitable fatalities. Nonetheless, this led the young warriors to believe that they could take on the Tompiki head on, and they were itching to do just that.

They learned to use the bow and arrows captured from the Tompiki as well as the deadly machetes. They trained with these so regularly that in time, these became their secondary weapons. All throughout their training, the youth never saw Kahuru, although it was a known fact that he was their main overseer, and they knew that he was always watching them from a distance. Sometimes, he would appear at their camp at dead of night to talk briefly to Makaba before vanishing into the night.

The training went on like that, intensifying with every day that passed. By the beginning of the second moon, the regiment was isolated from the rest of the army. At this time, training included very complex evolutions in rapid order, the technique of close fighting devised by Kahuru, war games, and maneuvers with blunted weapons.

If Makaba was feared for his driving and bitter tongue lashings, he was also loved for his care for the youth's wellbeing: "Do I want to see you eaten by vultures and hyenas after the next war merely because you were too stupid or lazy to understand that what I am trying to teach you, today, may save your lives, tomorrow?"

It was to reasons known only to Kahuru why this particular regiment was being subjected to such gruesome training. The youth became such fierce fighters that the Nguni people from the South, who inhabited the land between the great Drakensburg Mountains and the sea, nicknamed the regiment *Thambo la Nyonga*—bone of a snake. The Sotho-Tswana, who spoke a different dialect, but like the Nguni also pledged allegiance to king Swathi, called them *Sapo la Noga*. The meaning being the same, but which somehow conveyed an impression of strength.

Kahuru, himself, conducted the final phase of their training. The youth had not been notified beforehand, so it was with great shock and surprise when they were awoken earlier than usual and ordered to assemble at the training field within the blink of an eye. They arrived, expecting to find Makaba ready to bark orders at them. Instead,

Kahuru was amidst the early morning mist that covered the forest. He was surrounded by five fully-grown leopards. This sight alone made the entire regiment shudder with awe and fear. What made the surprise worse was that some of the youth were witnessing this phenomenon in person for the very first time. The human leopard always chose to be inconspicuous whenever opportunity allowed.

The youth immediately stood in a well-practiced formation and were just about to hail praise and greetings at Kahuru when, instead, the immortal raised his spear above his head, telling the warriors to keep their mouths shut.

The human leopard gazed at the regiment assembled in silence before him. He recognized many of them, and with glowing eyes in the semi darkness, he approached the silent brigade. He took time to inspect the entire regiment with a look that made some of the warriors wonder if indeed, they had full control over their bladders. It did not matter how much rigorous training of mind, body, and spirit they were subjected to, nothing had prepared them for this. Kahuru was frightening even for his people.

To his delight, he noticed that every warrior seemed comfortable with their secondary weapons. The blacksmiths in the land, as a matter of state emergency, had been ordered to manufacture replicas of the Tompiki arsenal.

Considering the little time   they were given; they had done a magnificent job and thus, would be rewarded accordingly by the king and his council of elders.

Following his rather intense inspection of the regiment, Kahuru strode to the front and faced the warriors once more. Being quite tall, he could be seen by even the shortest warrior in the rear. All this time, the leopards had not moved an inch and seemed to take no note of the humans. In a fierce and inhumane voice, Kahuru began by saying,

"Men of the *Thambo la Nyonga* regiment, it is good to see that you have been trained well and are thus, ready for war. I will begin by telling you why this regiment was assembled. Our main army needs a special unit that will make its job easier. You were chosen mainly because you are at the threshold of manhood and hence, eager to prove your worth. You have no wives, children, compounds, or even livestock. In short, you have no responsibilities except to yourselves."

At that juncture, Kahuru paused and gazed at the men for a long time to see if the men were listening—they were spellbound.

"The question you are probably all asking yourselves is what your mission is. The answer is simple, great warriors. To ensure total victory, we will always have to be on the offensive, constantly harassing the Tompiki with night raids capped by total aggression. Our responsibility will be to make this war as uncomfortable for them as possible, softening them, so to speak, and laying ground for our main army to add the finishing blows." Kahuru was in fact anticipating over a century and a half, a series commando of raids; 'hit and run' tactics employed in modern day guerilla warfare.

"It is necessary to add that this is a very dangerous task. Many of you will not come back. But remember this always—We never die!"

Following his speech, the ground vibrated as the 5,000 warriors roared like thunder as they stamped their feet on the ground. With the enthusiasm and joy common to youth, many were eager to outdo the other; they were itching for personal glory under Kahuru's command. It was every young man's dream to be named 'Great' before reaching the age of twenty-five. The land had known of only one such unprecedented achievement, and that was when Tladi, the son of Ndaba, the poet and orator, was named such many seasons earlier.

It now took little effort to subject the youth to the final strenuous field training. This time, it was under the direct supervision of Kahuru, himself; for the next seven days, the human leopard added ten more miles to their daily forty to fifty mile jog trot. A culmination on battle maneuvers in addition to hit and run guerrilla warfare were the order of the day. The same could be said about the main impi under the command of king Swathi of the Bakhudung, and king Morobe of the Bafokeng. In these route marches, any warrior who fell out without just and sufficient reason was instantly relegated to those who were assigned to guard the women, children, livestock, and grain still hidden in various parts of the great forests that bounded the Bakhudung.

These men would later not be regarded as real men but as closer in rank to their women folk. Since this title was worse than death, such instances were few and far between. Thus, an army was born that would either defeat the Tompiki or die.

Kahuru was faced with one major task. He needed a small band of men to spy incessantly on the Tompiki in attempt to know the day-to-day activities of their enemies. This was going to be a dangerous assignment, most certainly a suicide mission, and the human leopard was not prepared to sacrifice any of his men. The spies would have to be men who had nothing to lose and would not be entirely missed by the village in the unfortunate event that they lost their lives. But then, who would these people be? He decided to talk to king Swathi about this paradox that very evening.

The solution came from a much unexpected angle. After secretly meeting up with the king, Kahuru voiced his problem; Swathi listened and pondered for a while. After doing so, he smiled at the immortal and said,

"Do you remember Pongoza?"

"Of course, he was a great warrior. May the ancestors protect him in the spirit world," the human leopard replied.

"You know that Pongoza beget five children?"

"Yes, Zweli, Sizwe, Thabo, and Dala, the name of the fifth one, the daughter, still eludes me." The Oracle had told him about them.

"Quite right, great warrior, and as you know, those lads committed a heinous offence and as a result, were banished from the village. They then turned out to be "killers of the night" or better known as the "vulture brothers," who have terrorized hunters for quite some time now."

"Yes, and it is believed that they were responsible for the deaths of three of Mapoulo's men even though that story is not well authenticated for lack of solid proof."

Swathi's face was all surprise. He was used to Kahuru's proverbial accuracy, yet every instance of it surprised and impressed him.

"So you understand where I am heading at now, don't you? The king asked.

"Yes," he nodded, "let us use them as spies. The land can do without them if they end up dead," Kahuru added coldly.

"That will be their punishment." Swathi agreed. "And if for some reason they succeed, we might consider granting them a pardon for their crimes and lifting their banishment."

"That is true, great king. I will leave tonight, find them, and make them an offer they will dare not refuse," Kahuru said as he stood up getting ready to leave.

"Do you know where to find them great, warrior?"

"Yes, I may just know exactly where to find them." He had already vanished into the darkness via the opened door of the royal hut. *Did this man ever tire?* Swathi wondered to himself as he shrugged his massive shoulders.

And that was how Kahuru overcame the last stumbling block in their preparation for the forthcoming war. It had not been difficult to locate the four brothers turned brigands. After taking them by complete surprise in dramatic fashion, Kahuru told them exactly what he wanted from them. They were to watch the Tompiki at close proximity and find out their weaknesses, most importantly, the moments at which night raids would be most effective. Having gathered this information, they were to report in person to the human leopard on a daily basis. If they failed to do so, he was going to subject them to the slowest and most painful death known, and the brothers believed him.

Fleeing the land was out of question. Kahuru would trek them down even if it meant employing his leopards and the rest in the wild, not necessarily under his command. Incidentally, he had made sure to bring along his very own, so as to further validate his threats. Besides, as he himself put it, the brigands left behind a trail that even a blind man could follow.

After securing the brothers services, Kahuru secretly met with them every night. The brothers did a good job, nonetheless. They stuck to their end of the deal by spying incessantly on the Tompiki. Even though they did not fully understand the Tompiki language, they were able to pick on vital information.

An able general led the entire Tompiki army, which stood at 31,000 men. He was a mountain of a man named Walumbi, who was tough and ruthless. He was extremely bitter over the loss at Rolong and would have carried out daylight raids on the Bakhudung if the Tompiki elders had not opposed him. They had to approach this war with extreme caution now. What worried them were the reports that their enemies employed supernatural powers and that they were led by a man who looked like a man and a leopard at the same time.

It was said that this being possessed a spear that flew back to his palm after the target was met, not to mention the fact that he had the strength and endurance equal to that of a buffalo. For those who had not yet seen this phenomenon, they dismissed this story as nonsense. But according to those who lived to tell the story of the battle of Rolong, the best move would be to flee the land and never come back. Nothing on this green earth would entice them to fight again.

Walumbi labeled these men as cowards and traitors to their cause. He would show them that not only did such a creature not exist; he, himself, would cut the head clean off the man who masqueraded as a human leopard, and drink from his skull. In the end, he would carry the majority with him.

The land of the Bakhudung boasted of riches beyond imagination. They would have to take the land away by force and turn the natives into their slaves. Then, many seasons of wandering would be over. With that, the warriors sharpened their knives and filled the quivers with arrows, and some of the enthusiasm shown before the battle of Rolong returned. They were now ready to invade the Bakhudung in two days.

By this time, Kahuru had perfected his news carrier service to such an extent that whatever happened in "Tompiki land" was known to him in less than a day. So when he heard that the Tompiki were ready to march on them within two days, the human leopard met with his generals and mobilized the entire infantry battalion—all 25,000 of them.

The day before the war was when the army gathered at the arena in front of their four commanders, Kahuru, Morobe, Makaba, and Swathi, who gave a fine speech that was to be remembered for generations to come. In brief, he talked about how their livelihood and the peace that they had worked so hard to preserve were at stake. This was their fatherland, and no strangers were going to drive them out of it, no matter how big or small.

He ended by saying that the Tompiki were bloodthirsty and that they (the unified army) were going to make them swim in their own blood. He also reiterated that the Tompiki were full of fire after the battle of Rolong. It was now their chance to fight fire with fire. Deafening war cries drowned the rest of Swathi's words. That day, the ground literally shook as 25,000 feet stamped in unison.

Meanwhile, the elite unit known as *Thambo la Nyonga* or *Sapo la Noga* that was handpicked by Kahuru and Morobe had already assumed its battle position, which was some ten miles north along the great Mfolozi River and was awaiting Kahuru's return in the night time.

CHAPTER 17

BY NOON OF THE THIRD DAY, close to half of the unified army took its position at "the veld of death." It was named such because it was the same scene where the first Tompiki regiment under the command of Bamwa had succumbed. The place was still littered with white bones. The Bakhudung hoped the white bones would instill a negative psychological effect on their enemies.

Kahuru's secret service had worked so well that a day before the Tompiki's marched from their settlement, he had evacuated all the non-fighters within a radius of forty miles. These non-fighters were old men, women, children, and the young maidens whose sole duty was to see to it that the army was well tended to in terms of food, clothing, and equipment. There was no game in sight as the Bakhudung had already taken care of that.

Morobe was named commander of this army, which anxiously awaited the arrival of the invaders. The rest of the army, under the direct command of Swathi and Makaba, was scattered around the surrounding forest. Shortly after noon, two young men were seen running mightily towards the awaiting army. Their faces were flushed, and dust covered their feet right up to their knees. They were out of breath by the time they reached King Morobe at the forefront.

The two men immediately halted and bowed cordially at the Bafokeng king. He had been expecting them because they were the unified army's scouts.

"How far?" Morobe asked immediately.

"Less than a mile, O king," one of the scouts managed to say amidst a series of rapid pants.

"They stand tall and strong. It looks like it's their entire army, just as the mighty Kahuru had said," the second scout added. He, too, was fighting for breath.

"About how many?" Morobe asked again. His features were calm for a man who was about to lead his men to one of the most intense and gruesome war Africa has ever known, greater even, than the war with the outcasts.

The scout looked around at the vast regiment that was standing at ease but ready to pounce at the earliest command.

"I would say about seven to one if this is the regiment that will take them head on."

Again, the human leopard's estimation had not been far off, and this impressed Morobe even more.

"Good, you both have done a great job. Go back to the village and rest; I will send for you later."

"Thank you, great king."

The two men had been up all night standing guard. Their duty was to immediately report the first signs of a Tompiki march.

Morobe issued instructions to the man standing next to him who, in turn, told another, and in no time, the 7,500 men under Morobe's command assumed their famous battle formation. Poised with a large shield and three light throwing spears, each man took two giant steps forward. Thereafter all warriors counted five paces away from one another. The whole drill lasted a few seconds and looked as if one man performed it.

"The men are ready, great king," Morobe's most senior lieutenant announced shortly.

"Good, I bet we will not wait long."

And no sooner had he said that when there was a cloud of dust visible from the north. The Tompiki had arrived at last, all 31,000 of them; clad in full war gala. The two armies stood half a mile from each other. The Tompiki were led by a muscular man who stood at seven-foot and two inches (over 2 meters). His face was painted in patterns of red and white ochre, which distinguished him from the rest of his men—Walumbi.

The number and size of the Tompiki made Morobe and his men shudder. This, indeed, was a threat from another world. For a long time, nothing happened as both armies stared at each other. Morobe's army was vastly outnumbered, but Walumbi was not fooled. He knew that the rest of the army was hiding somewhere in the surrounding forest. To prevent a deadly ambush, he had already assigned 10,000 warriors to guard the rear by facing the opposite direction.

Upon seeing what the Tompiki were up to, Morobe raised a loud hoop, and at once, his army raised their large shields, which were so compact and light that they could be handled with one hand. Following that command, the unified army began its battle chant and stamped their right feet in unison. Walumbi, on the other hand, shouted instructions at his men that were then passed on to the rear. And suddenly, about 8,000 Tompiki marched forward to dare the unified army's challenge. Their bows were extended, and they seemed to be aiming at the sky. Morobe wondered why and knew that he was about to find out.

When they were fifty yards away, the Tompiki warriors came to a sudden halt. As this pause grew longer, Morobe wondered if they were waiting for him to attack. That would mean radically altering his plan, an idea he did not like. He ordered his men to somewhat relax. The next instant, the battle chant intensified, for the Tompiki were advancing, again. They came on boldly, with their bows very much extended this time.

As soon as they were within shooting range, the Tompiki sent the first volley of arrows at the chanting army. These arrows were shot high up in the sky, and Morobe and his men stared in horror as they came showering at them like rain. Many warriors were mortally hit before they could adequately shield themselves. Morobe immediately understood why their enemies aimed their projectiles at the sky. When shot way up, the arrows came down with ferocious speed, power, and accuracy, which made them hard to defend against unlike if they were shot straightforward, where they would be met by a wall of shields.

"Crouch on your heels with your shields above your heads," Morobe shouted.

Right at that instant, another volley of arrows was sent, but this time, his men were prepared for the assault. Many of the arrows just bounced harmlessly off the shields. Immediately thereafter, Morobe let out another hoop, and the first five columns of his men (about 5,000 of them) immediately stood up and answered with a volley of their own. Since the Tompiki carried no shields as these were foreign to them, their bodies were very exposed, meaning that many at the forefront were at the mercy of the unified army's spears. Morobe's men immediately sat on their heels, and the last three columns at the rear rushed forward to take the lead and hurled more spears at the enemy, who were rather slow in countering the previous attack. This time, an even larger number of them fell. The Tompiki were stunned.

At that moment, Walumbi shouted and the remaining Tompiki retreated and joined the rest of the army. Morobe's men wanted to follow, but their commander refrained them with much difficulty. They were like wild dogs on a leash, but orders were orders. Both armies increased the distance between them and paused for a while to lick their wounds.

They did not have to wait long because Walumbi ordered his warriors to form three long columns. The first sent a shower of arrows and immediately made way for the second unit, who with bare machetes, gave vent to a terrible war cry and charged. There were over 10,000 of them. Morobe immediately ordered his warriors to send another volley of spears, and the Tompiki fell in droves. Yet still, the remaining Tompiki advanced with a passion. Their faces were twisted in a horrible grin. Another volley met them, and more fell to the earth. This second assault made them somewhat pause, allowing fresher warriors from the second column to replace their dead and wounded comrades. At that moment, Morobe grasped what Walumbi's intentions were. The Tompiki general was sacrificing a portion of his vast army to enable him to close in on Morobe's fighters. This would mean close combat, which the unified army was not equipped to handle. And sure as the sun would rise the next day, they would be annihilated.

That was when the Bafokeng king sounded the retreat. This retreat was quickly carried out. The unified army turned and fled into the rear forest, just as the menacing Tompiki were barely one hundred yards away. They gave chase but quickly gave up on the idea not too far into the forest. Walumbi's instructions were clear; they were not to be sucked into the forest and then led into a deadly ambush. This maneuver had caused many lives, a lesson learned at Rolong. They were first going to familiarize themselves with this new territory before they launched an all-out offensive, which would mainly include hunting the enemy down to the last man in their stronghold—the forest. Needless to say, they did, in that brief charge, manage to overtake some of the fleeing warriors, who did not run fast enough, and mow them down savagely.

The spirited Tompiki reluctantly gave up the chase and returned to the rest of the army. Many still wanted to go after Morobe and his men. They were furious about the heavy losses they had suffered, and they felt that all-out war was necessary and that the time was now. They were willing to dare the enemy in their stronghold.

Many were vocal about their views, and it took Walumbi a while to restore order. They needed to be more tactful if they were to win this war, he had said time and again. The Bakhudung and their allies had proven to be able fighters. If they followed them into the forest, the Tompiki would be doing exactly what the enemy wanted them to do, fighting their war.

"What should be done then?" One of Walumbi's captains asked.

"Give me time to think about it. In the meantime, let us tend to the dead and wounded and then eat before dusk sets in."

The Tompiki had brought over a hundred head of cattle with them, some of which were slaughtered and roasted over hundreds of small fires. The food was heavily rationed as the Tompiki were not taking anything for granted. For all they knew, it would be days before they captured any more cattle. There was a serious omission, though, and it did not take long before they realized it.

"What shall we do for water?" A young captain by the name of Jola asked.

"What happened to the one we brought?" Walumbi wanted to know. It was Jola who was placed in charge of the drinking water.

"It's almost finished and needs to be replenished." Then as an afterthought, Jola added. "Maybe the wells from that deserted village would do."

The "deserted village" was the now dilapidated village of the Barolong, scarcely five miles away.

"Obviously, you don't seem to be laboring under the heavy burden of brains do you? Those wells have been poisoned," the giant Tompiki snapped.

"What then do you suggest?"

"The rivers, of course; send a heavy patrol to fetch water."

The river Walumbi was talking about was close to ten miles north east of where they were. Immediately afterwards, a unit of 6,000 men was assembled and ready to dispatch. It was already late in the afternoon, and they knew that they had to get to the river before sunset. With Jola in command, the Tompiki set off to the river. They were instructed to be on the lookout for any surprise attacks on the way.

Morobe met king Swathi in the depths of the forest at a place known as Khotsong, a place that was once the outcast's infamous fortress. The place had since been purified of its evil through numerous rites. The Bafokeng king was showered with praise following his first encounter with the Tompiki at the veld of death. Things had gone according to plan. Morobe's 7,500 men suffered 800 casualties with less than 50 seriously wounded, compared to the 1,800 suffered by the Tompiki. Kahuru's strategy had worked to near perfection.

The human leopard had assigned Morobe the task of leading 7,500 warriors to meet the Tompiki at the veld of death. The plan was simple, yet effective. With the skill of vanishing into the forest at a moment's notice, Morobe's men were to lure the Tompiki into a fierce fight even though they were vastly outnumbered; the idea was to test the strength of the Tompiki when it came to straight up conventional warfare. That objective was achieved. The Tompiki were not only fierce and strong fighters, they were also very brave and were willing to sacrifice many lives if they could close in on their foes and employ the deadly machetes. These machetes were so razor thin sharp that they could cut the head or limb clean off any man with ease as seen at the most recent battle.

This meant that when it came to close combat, the Bakhudung and the unified army stood little or no chance against this main Tompiki threat. The main Bakhudung tactic was going to be guerrilla warfare, the objective being to rapidly cut the number of the giants and dampen their morale, in the process, unleashing unto them man's deadliest enemy—fear.

After the wounded were tended to and the warriors fed, Morobe and Swathi went into the latter's temporary hut and spoke in low tones. They were obviously discussing the next offensive tactic. Talks of this nature were highly surreptitious and sensitive. Anybody not at the top chain of command was not allowed anywhere near the generals when they were engaged in meetings such as these because as Swathi, put it: 'The trees have ears.'

The main question at the moment was what the human leopard had in mind. None of the warriors at Khotsong, Morobe and Swathi included, had seen him, Makaba, the *Thambo la Nyonga*, and the Buffalo regiments since that morning, but they all knew that whatever the two were planning was major. Kahuru had made sure that messengers informed the two kings of his presence somewhere in the forest and to immediately notify him if immediate help was needed.

After the meeting between the two generals, some 3,000 warriors were ordered to spread out in the vicinity and stand guard while the rest stretched out on the forest floor and rested. Meanwhile, the two kings, Swathi and Morobe, awaited the human leopard's return. They expected him that evening.

Jola and his 6,000 men reached the banks of the great river at twilight after a long and hard march. The march through the forest went without incident, much to their pleasant surprise. Although, they heard footsteps scampering away once or twice, enemy scouts no doubt. But, Jola sought comfort in the fact that their number was staggering, and a small regiment would not dare attack them.

The Tompiki approached the great, gentle, flowing river with caution. This section of the river was broad, and the setting sun behind them lit that stretch of water like a theater stage. The river was a bright, emerald green, with the papyrus beds crowned with gold where the sunrays struck them.

Jola raised his hand, his assistants followed suit, and the entire army took cover amidst the trees and shrubs of the forest. In a low voice, he ordered 200 men to go to the river and scour the surroundings. The warriors came back after a while. There was no evident danger. The surroundings looked safe and sound.

Jola was not fully satisfied. He ordered more scouts to scour the surroundings in an attempt to locate the enemy. The scouts came back with the same report. There was not a soul in sight. On the other side of the river was a cliff. He gazed at the top for a while, wondering if their enemies were hiding up there waiting to pounce on them. He quickly dismissed the thought; an attack from that position would not be effective and thus, not be feasible.

In the end, Jola convinced himself that they were too far away from the enemy, so an attack was less likely. Moments later, the Tompiki were filling the goatskin gourds with water. They formed many columns of men who filled their containers and passed it on to the next man and so on. After a while, the tension wore off and gave way to some singing and merriment; that is, before the peace was disrupted by a terrifying war cry.

This war cry was followed by thousands more as the stunned Tompiki looked around like caged animals. Before they could react, hundreds upon hundreds of arrows showered on them like a tropical rainfall. The missiles seemed to be coming from everywhere, even from the overhead cliff that earlier seemed to pose no threat at all.

By the time the Tompiki countered with their own volley, almost a quarter of them lay dead or seriously injured. There were two questions that struck Jola at once. Why had he not foreseen this? Only a fool would not have sensed a trap. And how was it that the enemy employed the same weapons as them: the bow and arrows? These, indeed, were formidable opponents. Perhaps they should have listened to the fighters who had suggested earlier on that the campaign against the Bakhudung be abandoned shortly after the massacre at Rolong.

Just as Jola sounded the retreat, thousands of the Bakhudung emerged from the surrounding forest. These warriors were armed with large shields and spears. They were Kahuru and Makaba's elite; the feared *Thambo la Nyonga* or *Sapo la Noga* brigade.

The nation's elite unit's war chant rolled like rumbling thunder across the forest. With the beginning of the chant, the speed of this unit slowed down to the rhythmic measured jog trot of a death dance as they closed in on the Tompiki. And at every tenth step, there was an earth-shaking stamp of the right foot, carried out with perfect unison by all. To the Tompiki's utter dismay, they saw the Bakhudung warriors unsheathe long machetes from behind their shields. There was a deadly silence for the time required to take a deep breath. Then the fearful war Bakhudung war cry crashed out, "*Aieee*," and the *Sapo la Noga* brigade charged.

With the large shields protecting their bodies and their ability to wield their machetes with above average dexterity, this Bakhudung unit had all odds in their favor. The fact that the Tompiki were forced to fight with their backs to the great river put them at a critical disadvantage. The clash of bodies against shields was deafening as both sides fought to the death. The Tompiki fought even more desperately, and it was through sheer will and determination that they managed to open a gap in their enemies' formidable battle formation. But, this did not come without a great loss of lives. Chief lost among these gallant Tompiki warriors was Jola.

With his bare machete, he would duck under an intended death blow (by crouching to his heels), grab at the enemy's shield with his free hand, and drive home his bare machete on the exposed side of his man before repeating this maneuver time and again.

However, they were faced by a better-trained and better-skilled army that moved swiftly with its shields, machetes, and spears. Before long, many of the Tompiki took to the river. Some drowned or were too wounded to swim and because of such, that portion of the river quickly turned red with blood. It did not take long for nearby crocodiles to close in on a hefty feast.

Within a short space of time, it was all over. The Tompiki who had not been killed had been pushed into or taken by the river. Only a very few, about 300 of them, had managed to escape on foot. Among them was Jola. They did not run in a group, but instead, scattered around the forest. This stupendous achievement had caused the

Bakhudung's elite less than 1,000 men. The regiments regrouped and awaited Kahuru's return. It was almost night time. The wounded were tended to, and those not strong enough to stand or even walk, were carried to Khotsong, where extra care was administered. The other battalion under Makaba, the Buffalo unit, close to 8,000 of them covered the ford in a compact body.

The *Thambo la Nyonga* awaited Kahuru because with him, came the final phase of the war.

CHAPTER 18

KAHURU HAD WITNESSED the entire battle from the cliff top on the other side of the great river. The Bakhudung's elite had been magnificent to such an extent that his presence was not needed at all. All they had to do was follow his instructions and listen to the chief drill instructor, Makaba, at all times. But, the human leopard knew that the war was far from over in spite of this splendid victory. He wanted to end it that very night if possible.

Through his spies, Kahuru found out that the rest of the Tompiki army was still camped at the veld of death, awaiting the return of Jola and his unit. That was when Kahuru realized his chance for total victory and immediately sent word to Khotsong, informing the two generals, Swathi and Morobe, to mobilize the rest of the army under their command and to march quietly towards the veld of death.

He sent word further on to the elite unit to stand by and await the arrival of a new general who was to carry out the final command. This man was to be obeyed without question since he would be representing Kahuru, himself. The same message was relayed to Makaba, who was still in charge of the Buffalo regiment that still stood guard along the fords of the great river. Their main objective was to stop the Tompiki if they decided to come back for water under the cover of darkness.

This latest development startled and surprised the young men. Who was this mysterious commander who was to lead them on a possible night raid? Where was Kahuru, or rather, what would he be doing all this time? This was bizarre. The youth were caught in a nest of questions without answers. They felt naked without him, but nonetheless, they waited patiently. The moon had already risen, and the warriors knew they would have to wait for it to set before any attack could be initiated. That would be shortly after midnight.

The youth of the *Thambo la Nyonga* waited silently. No fire was lit. Only streaks of light from the full moon, which cut through the thick foliage overhead, gave light. For a long time, nothing happened. The men's eyelids grew heavy and sticky as they tried to blink themselves to alertness. Then suddenly, one of the lookout men came back.

"Someone is coming," he whispered excitedly at Fasimba, the same Fasimba who was assigned with three other colleagues to find Tladi in the forest. He was among the first to be handpicked by Makaba and Kahuru to form this elite regiment.

"Is it Kahuru, the leopard man?

"No," the lookout man replied. "It's a tall, young man with a majestic stride that comes."

Fasimba's heart started beating fast. Who could that be? Was it the mysterious stranger they had been warned to be on the lookout for? No one could tell.

"Are you sure it is only one man that approaches?" the youth wanted to know.

"Absolutely," the lookout man replied.

At that moment, Fasimba made a sound similar to that of a night bird, and instantaneously, every single man dove for cover as silent as a slithering snake through grass—all 3,700 of them! One can never fully emphasize how well trained these men were. Shortly thereafter, a tall, young man emerged from an unexpected angle. He was armed with a shield and three long spears. He walked with the grace and confidence of a Great, and just like them, he was clad in full war gala.

The young man paused for a while and laid down his weapons, save for the short-throwing knobkerrie fastened to his waist. He looked like a fellow clansman and high-ranking commander from the way he was dressed. But then who was he? From his hiding place, Fasimba could not discern who the intruder was. Yet, at the same time, the walk, the posture, and figure looked very familiar.

"Men of the elite unit known as *Thambo la Nyonga* or *Sapo la Noga*, I hereby announce my arrival to oversee the final phase of this war." A booming voice from the intruder's cavernous chest broke the cold silence of the night. Up to that point, even the typical sounds of the night seemed to have stopped as if waiting for this dramatic moment.

Fasimba's veins pounded with fast flowing blood. The same could be said about the rest. What they were hearing seemed improbable. *Could this be?* ... Instead, he decided to speak up.

"Who goes there? Speak up and speak up now." Although he tried to hide it, there was a nervous ring in his voice. Only the human leopard could have this effect on him, not a mere mortal; or so he thought.

"I am Tladi, the son of Ndaba, the poet and orator of the Bakhudung."

There was a long and audible gasp that seemed to come from everywhere, the trees, the leaves, and the grass as every warrior expressed his utter shock and amazement. Although they had been trained to react appropriately and swiftly to any surprise, nothing had prepared them for this. It took longer than usual for the astonishing news to sink in.

"Tladi?" is it really you … but how? … Where is the human leopard?" Fasimba managed to ask.

"Yes it is I, Tladi, son of Ndaba. You men show yourselves at once. We have a lofty task ahead of us."

It was a command, and everybody obeyed. A long lost warrior and leader had returned. Slowly, the warriors emerged from all corners of the forest. There was a loud murmur as everybody tried to make sense of the whole situation. Tladi, the son of Ndaba, the poet and orator, but how was that possible? No one could make the connection between him and Kahuru.

A fire was lit immediately. Yes, it was, indeed, the long lost warrior whom the Bakhudung and the rest of the nations that knew him held in high esteem. That is, of course, if we exclude the immortal that was a half-man half-beast. Some even went to the extent of touching him just to make sure that the man standing before them was, indeed, a mortal and not a spirit. It took a while to bring the men to order.

"Men of the elite unit," Tladi addressed the warriors as he stood on the other side of the bomb fire, whose tongues seemed to be reaching for the very high foliage. "There is no time to waste. We are to advance on the Tompiki, tonight, and…."

"Pardon me, great warrior, but where is the leopard man? I believe I speak for …" A warrior from the Barolong people interrupted.

"Silence!" Tladi's voice cracked like a whip. "And let me not hear anymore interruptions. Save your questions until the war is over." After making certain that he had been well understood, the warrior continued by saying,

"I will lead 200 men who will sneak with me right into the belly of the Tompiki army. Our objective is to cause full-scale panic and confusion among them. The rest of you will wait on a possible ambush following the chaos we hope to create. The 200 men will have to be as tall or taller than I am, men who could easily be mistaken as one of the Tompiki in the dark. Now who will those men be?"

He had barely finished asking the question when eager hands went up immediately.

"This is a daring mission that requires men with ice in their veins. Anything can go wrong, and we may end up being captured and killed," the warrior warned.

Again, eager youths came surging forward. Their well-formed muscles rippled as they elbowed one another. It was difficult to choose. It took a little while, but in the end, he was able to pick his men, among them Fasimba, whom he rather liked. Afterwards, he went over his plan, again and again, until he was satisfied that everybody understood what his duties were. It had not been difficult to capture their full attention. He did, after all, speak in straightforward and effective language, similar in many ways to Kahuru. It was as if their immortal was there with them in mind and in spirit.

With Tladi and his 200 men at the forefront, the *Thambo la Nyonga* regiment silently jog trotted the ten-mile distance to the veld of death. When they were within the vicinity of the enemy encampment, the regiment paused to catch their breath, after which, Tladi went over his plan one final time. They were facing the veld coming from the north. Tladi went on to inform them that the rest of the army under king Swathi, king Morobe, and the ever courageous Makaba had secured the area south, east, and west, respectively. In essence, it meant that the Tompiki were completely surrounded without them knowing it.

Thereafter, Tladi and his men smeared their bodies with some dark, slimy clay that they had brought along, their intention to camouflage their features as much as possible. With thumping hearts, for this was a vicious gamble, the men discarded their shields. Armed only with long spears capped by wide blades, which could not be distinguished from machetes in the darkness, the 200 men led by Tladi strode towards the Tompiki encampment. The Tompiki had not lit any fires for fear of being easy targets for their enemies who were lurking somewhere in the surrounding forest. Tladi and his men walked like people on the retreat, with the hope that they would be mistaken as part of the unit that had been sent to fetch water from the Mfolozi.

Walumbi learned about the ambush at the Mfolozi from the first band of fugitives, who arrived shortly after dusk. The men vividly described how they were led into a deadly trap. One warrior went on to explain how the natives made them feel as though that particular area had been as safe as their backyards.

"The amazing thing," the warrior said, "was that all the way to the river, there were no indications that the enemy was lurking somewhere in the vicinity with their entire army, save for the few scouts here and there. We made it a point to scour the area within a two-mile radius very thoroughly. But just at the moment when we thought that we were safe from an attack, we got hit fast and hard. What was even worse is that the natives are employing our same weapons against us. Part of them, at least," the warrior added.

This bit of news startled and sickened Walumbi to the stomach. For the very first time since the invasion, he began to feel waves of trepidation. These were no ordinary people they were facing. Worse still was that their food supply was running to a critical low. Sooner or later, they would be goaded by hunger and mainly thirst. After ensuring that the food was heavily rationed, he ordered his men to rest. They would advance to one of the nearby villages at dawn in an attempt to replenish their almost depleted food supply. Fragments of Jola's troop were still arriving at regular intervals, but Jola, himself, was still at large.

When Tladi and his men arrived, nobody paid them any particular notice. They were merely asked if they were being followed, and the inquirer was simply answered with a grunt. The men took their positions amongst the sleeping Tompiki as cautiously as they could without arousing suspicion. The men Tladi picked could not afford to be clumsy as this would certainly cause them their lives. Each warrior lay down next to a sleeping Tompiki and awaited the signal. They did not have to wait long.

Presently, a piercing yell awoke the veld, followed by similar yells everywhere as the Bakhudung slayers began their deadly work. In a moment, pandemonium broke loose, and hundreds of hand-to-hand encounters took place, principally among the Tompiki themselves. The Bakhudung had practically each gotten his man and had then evaded the action by a pretense of death, lying still beside each corpse. After the first sharp tumult was over, a general truce automatically succeeded it, in which, each Tompiki sat down and suspiciously regarded his neighbor, whom at best he could dimly see.

The tense situation had continued for a time when inquiries were shouted from Walumbi's headquarters and relayed by further shouts to the confines of the encampment. Confused reports came back in the same way, which only heightened the bewilderment of all ranks. All agreed that there had been no general or organized attack, and yet death had smitten them from within. Some evil sorcery was abroad, for friend had killed friend.

Walumbi gave orders that twigs and branches should be collected and piled up to light the camp. No sooner had the Tompiki moved to carry out this command, when the death yells filled the night air, and the fuel collecting ceased immediately. These indistinguishable death dealers petrified the Tompiki, who, though never afraid of the normal, were completely cowed by the abnormal. Some went as far as saying they were being struck by the spirits of their dead comrades, who had succumbed at that same veld not too long before.

As resourceful and brave a man as he was, Walumbi ordered all the Tompiki forth to concentrate and mass around his headquarters, which was his makeshift hut, and to keep as close together as the undergrowth would permit.

A general movement on these lines now began, but shortly thereafter, in the rear of the outmost groups, the horrible death cries arose again. The Bakhudung killers mostly attached themselves to the tail end of the innumerable Tompiki groups, and as the groans and yells of the mortally stricken increased, a general rush for the headquarters rendezvous was inevitable.

When the Tompiki were all drawn fairly close together around Walumbi's headquarters, he ordered them to sit down and face outwards and called all the regimental and company commanders together for a report. Most of the evidence favored a supernatural occurrence, which, through vivid dreams or otherwise, had resulted in a fratricidal stabbing match.

There were some level-headed leaders, however, who felt fairly certain that the stabbing had been started by Bakhudung scouts who had penetrated into their midst. The question was now how to discover and ferret them out. That was, of course, assuming that they were still among them. Some 500 strong warriors were ordered, again, to seek dry twigs in the surrounding forest so that a useful number of effective fires could be made for identification purposes.

The moment these warriors began scouring the forest, they were met by numerous spears and arrows. Half of them barely escaped with their lives. The news was promptly reported back to Walumbi's headquarters. The enemy was everywhere, and without much thought, the Tompiki knew they were in the lion's den. It was not about winning the war and capturing the Bakhudung lands, anymore. It was about fighting for their lives.

Walumbi decided that they must wait until daylight. He then gave a bracing talk to his army, which was relayed by the captains sentence by sentence.

The Tompiki lay down and tried to sleep, but this was suddenly no easy matter after their recent alarming experience. Among them lay Tladi, the champion warrior the Bakhudung have known, very much alert and wondering how he would get out again before daylight brought his discovery. It had been the great oracle and sorcerer who had briefed him of this plan. He had appeared, in spirit form, to his alter ego, Kahuru, shortly after the ambush at Mfolozi. For this plan to succeed, he would have to be transformed to his human self. And once more, Kahuru had to travel that distance to the Oracle's caves and come back as Tladi.

For a while, Tladi lay still. After a period, when he judged the time to be ripe for action, he studied the dim outline of a warrior's body lying beside him and then sat up and delivered a mighty thrust into his chest. There was a gurgling scream from the stricken man. And in an instant, there was commotion among the Tompiki that was heightened by Tladi's screams, like one struck, which in fact was a signal to his men that the time was up. The Bakhudung sneaked away by crawling on their bellies over fifty yards until they were in the safety of the woods. They then rejoined their comrades, who showered them with praises—the screams from the Tompiki was like music to their ears.

The *Thambo la Nyonga* regiment had lost twenty-five men in that encounter. That was when they made a grim discovery. Tladi, the son of Ndaba, the poet and orator was missing. Fasimba was among the first to notice, but he was not unduly concerned. He knew the warrior would reappear someday just as suddenly as he had vanished.

Just before daybreak, Kahuru appeared dramatically before the awaiting elite unit. This time, his leopards accompanied him. The warriors immediately stood up and acknowledged his presence by quickly standing in a well-formed battle formation. Following the normal routine, the human leopard inspected each man before he took his position in front of them.

"The enemy has been severely wounded," he said. "They are tired, hungry, weak, and their morale is at an unprecedented low. They are surrounded, and now your day has come, men of the elite unit known as *Thambo la Nyonga*. Up! And destroy them all. Follow me!"

Amidst terrifying war cries, the bloodthirsty regiment followed the human leopard in full trot towards the Tompiki encampment. The latter were stunned to see this mass of men hurtling towards them at incredible speed, leaving a cloud of dust behind them. It was a surprise attack, and many of the Tompiki wondered if they would ever see the rising sun of the next day. They tried to repel or halt this attack by firing their arrows at will, but this had no effect, as more and more warriors joined in from all ends.

The Tompiki fought back like wounded lions, but their aggression was no match for a well-rested, well-equipped, and better fed army. Needless to say, hundreds of them were panic-stricken at the sight of Kahuru and his leopards. The arrows seemed to whiz past him as if he had an arrow-deflecting amulet in his possession.

The ease with which he grabbed his foes and ripped them to smithereens with his bare hands was frightening, not to mention the leopards that attacked the Tompiki men at will. Amidst this fierce clash, his aggression seemed to be directed towards the enormous Tompiki leader, Walumbi, who began retreating just at the mere sight of the immortal. After a short encounter, for the large Tompiki was no match for the human leopard, Kahuru incapacitated Walumbi by breaking his arms and legs. Shortly thereafter, he chopped off the Tompiki's head with his own machete and raised it for everyone amidst this fierce encounter to see. The sight was gruesome. Ironically, it was Walumbi who had promised his men that he would cut off clean the head of the man known as the human leopard or masquerading as such.

The big Walumbi was their leader. Having him dead was like crushing the head of a mamba, hence the entire Tompiki army or rather, most of them (because a few did manage to escape) succumbed to the spears and machetes of the Bakhudung and the rest of the unified army. With Kahuru, the leopards, and the two kings at the forefront, the Bakhudung and the unified army chased after the retreating Tompiki and were led to the Tompiki settlement that was overlooked by the *Lungile* escarpment. Here, every woman, child, elder, and dog was annihilated. Total victory was achieved, and with it, came the rebuilding process. Villages had been destroyed and some people scattered. But now, the war was over and what was left was for its wounds to heal.

Many seasons later, in 1794, the king's personal messenger named Morongwa walked into the royal hut and bowed cordially at the king. Swathi, now a much older man, looked at the young man whose eyes were wide with bewilderment and whose tongue seemed stuck to the roof of his mouth.

"Yes, what is it?" The king demanded. Despite his advanced age, he was still strong, and his eyes were fierce.

"T-there is a strange man who seeks your audience, O king. He speaks through an interpreter. He says he wishes to talk to you about Kahuru, the leopard man"

"Send him in," he said almost resignedly. He was used to dealing with such people who came from far and wide to ask about Kahuru. There was also the case of an imposter who almost succeeded in destroying the nation in more damaging ways than the Tompiki or the outcasts would have done, during which crisis, the whole nation had turned on Kahuru, branding him the enemy, but that is another story.

Shortly thereafter, Henry Thomas Davies walked into the royal hut with two other strangers after taking off his tricorn hat. King Swathi, who had never seen a white man this up close and personal before, almost jumped from his stool in shock and amazement, the same reaction he felt twenty-six seasons earlier when he saw Kahuru for the first time.

PART 3: THE AMERICAS

CHAPTER 19

BY 1789, THE PLANTATION OWNER known as Lloyd Benjamin Davies had amassed so much wealth, the full extent of which not even his wife could guess. Not only was he the chief producer of cotton, rice, and pecans, just to mention a few, in the entire state of Mississippi but also in the whole thirteen former colonies known now as states. One of his butlers developed a gin almost by accident, from cotton, which also helped to increase his cash flow. But, the bulk of his fortune came from a totally unexpected source, and not only did it make him rich but famous, too.

Sanza Kazadi, known now as Melvin Davies, was a twenty seven year old man. Henry Thomas Davies, son of Lloyd and Sara Davies, was twenty. The two had forged a friendship that had broken all sacred laws that forbade intimate associations between blacks and whites. At first, Lloyd Davies was so furious about this unusual friendship that he had, on several occasions, threatened to sell Sanza off to a plantation far off, never to be seen or heard of again. But when his only son vowed to run off in search of his friend and never return to the plantation, Mr. Davies thought differently of the matter, and years later, he had his son to thank. The two had built a bond that no person could break. And the harder one tried, the stronger the bond became.

The bond was started by Sanza Kazadi's tale about a half-man half-leopard known as Kahuru, whom Sanza had seen with his own eyes, as he brought about peace and goodwill. From the time Sanza told his young friend about this remarkable being, a mental picture of Kahuru was indelibly painted in his mind. For many nights, Henry would sneak out of the plantation mansion through the upstairs window of his bedroom, climb down the wall overlooking the courtyard, and then make his way to the slave quarters. In there, he would snuggle up next to Sanza, and the latter would continue with his chronicle, nights on end.

In return, Henry schooled the slave into a world that was reserved only for white people. What astonished everybody, including Henry, was the fact that Sanza possessed brains that functioned beyond the realm of anyone's comprehension. To start with, he learned to speak English fluently within three months of his arrival from Africa. When Henry started teaching him the alphabets and simple sentence structures, Sanza could not only recite the letters verbatim on the first try, but he could write and structure sentences like someone who had many years of education. And that took him only one day. By the end of the week, he could read, understand, and even quote chapters and verses from the King James Bible.

One day, Henry announced that he was going to teach him arithmetic. By noon that day, Sanza was being bombarded with sums to which not even his teacher knew the answers, but upon looking them up and seeing that, indeed, all the answers were correct to the last decimal, the young Davies was mute with amazement.

"Say, Sanza," Henry one day said to him. He only addressed him by his true name when there was no one even remotely within hearing range. "What is twelve times twelve divided by seventeen minus eighty four subtracted by one hundred and two divided by two point five, eh? ... I bet you won't know the answer to that one now, would you?" Henry smiled mischievously.

He was seventeen at the time, and Sanza was twenty-four, and there had been talk lately that Henry might be sent to a school in the north, a university to be exact, known as Harvard in the State of Massachusetts.

Sanza twisted his neck this way and that way, scratched his cheek, and accepted the challenge.

"It is simple, young master ... negative thirty eight point eight."

Henry quickly rolled up his sleeve to consult. He had memorized the answer but had written it on his forearm just so he could be certain. It had taken him all night to figure it out. He could not believe it when he heard the correct answer.

"My goodness, Sanza, how do you do that?" He exclaimed after letting out a loud and long whistle.

"I don't know, young master. It just comes to me."

Henry just shook his head and walked away. This was unbelievable. No one of color was supposed to be that smart. He was always told that people of color, or niggers as they were known, possessed no brains. God put them on this earth to serve the white race. They were no better than mules except that they stood and walked on two feet. Henry Davies began to question these beliefs that had been instilled in him since childhood. If the African known as Melvin had such a retentive brain, then it was safe to assume that there was a being known as Kahuru. As unusual as it may sound, the young Davies held strong to that belief.

Not surprisingly, Sanza's duties were strictly in or around the Davies mansion. He rarely ever set foot at the fields. It was with little effort that Henry brainwashed him to a point that Sanza began adopting his master's mannerisms and habits such as speech and dress. The young Davies even toyed with the idea of taking Sanza with him to Boston in the Fall. However, two major obstacles stood firm in his path. Sanza was still a slave, hence "property" of Lloyd Davies, and traveling that great distance with a black man without proper documentation was as good as leading his friend to the gallows.

But he needed Sanza desperately, though, because a secret plan was manifesting itself in his mind, and the slave was to play a major role in it. He had told nobody of this, including Sanza. Perhaps he would go to Boston on his own and come back after completing part of his studies to secure the financial backing and support of some major newspapers in the country, which also happened to be in Boston.

With this thought in mind, Henry walked into the main living room of the mansion and sat in front of the family piano. It was situated on the eastern side of the room beside the stairway leading to the upstairs rooms. It was night time, and the living room was brightly lit by the magnificent candle chandelier that hung high above the ceiling, directly vertical to the first five steps of the stairway.

Henry stretched his arms and started playing Wolfgang Amadeus Mozart's first symphony. He had been playing that since the age of eight and had just recently been on the verge of mastering the tune. The sound of the piano rubbed and caressed his very soul. It was at this moment when he felt relaxed, his whole body light and soft like a feather as if he could walk on the clouds and feel like a titan. He began going over his plan in his mind for the millionth time.

"Would you mind if I tried, young master?" A voice interrupted his meditation. He whirled with a frown on his face. He did not like being disturbed when in this mood, but something about Sanza always had a calming effect on him.

"How long have you been standing there?" Henry asked a bit surprised.

"Long enough to like what I am hearing; now, would you mind if I tried?"

Henry looked at the African standing before him. He was tall and handsome, no doubt, with a great figure and posture even though he had lost most of the bulging muscles he once possessed when he first arrived at the plantation. He was wearing an old pair of shoes that once belonged to Henry, a shirt, and a jacket (one of his priceless possessions), which was already starting to crawl above his wrists. What really stigmatized his status as a slave on the Davies plantation was his pair of trousers. Every slave on the plantation was required to wear them at all times except on Sundays. They were made from hard cloth and held to the waist by a piece of string, which, as in Sanza's case, the loose end dangled a few inches above the crouch.

Henry laughed outright as all these observations became abundantly clear to him.

"You, Sanza…" At that moment, he realized his indiscretion and immediately caught himself. They were inside the house, now, and the walls have been known to have ears. "You, Melvin … think you can play the piano?" He laughed even more.

"I can try with your permission, young master," Sanza said. He was unfazed by Henry's ridicule.

"Be my guest," the young Davies said as he stood up, ushering the slave to the piano. He was convinced that he was about to witness one of the most comical episodes of his life.

Sanza stretched his arms and flexed his fingers before having a seat. He banged a few senseless notes, but Henry soon realized that after a little while there was some type of tune developing. And right there and then, Mozart's first symphony filled the house. It was as if one of the greatest composers the world has known was playing the piano that night in the Davies household.

Henry was speechless. He could hardly believe his ears. This was not real!

"Holy Mary Madonna, Mother of God!" The young man gasped, his face pale as if he had seen a ghost. He was almost short of breath as he stood wide-eyed with his mouth slightly agape.

He instantly whirled and ran up the flight of stairs, taking more than three steps at a time and shouting in a voice hardly recognizable as his.

"Mom ... Dad ... come quickly and see!" He burst into the master bedroom, forgetting to knock in the process and ready to wake his parents up. But there was no need; the couple was already awake and was seated upright on their bed, listening to the music. They were certain that their son had finally mastered the symphony.

"What is it, son?" Lloyd Davies asked. He had never seen the bewildered look on his son's face before.

"Yes, what's the matter, Henry?" Sara Davies reiterated on behalf of her husband. At that very moment, the elderly couple exchanged a puzzled look. The music was still playing, and yet, their son was upstairs with them. How was that possible?

"It's ... it's ... Sanza." Henry managed to say.

"Who?" The couple exclaimed at the same time.

"I mean, Melvin," Henry quickly said as blood returned to his face, replacing the pale mask he had just won.

"No, it can't be," Lloyd said as he quickly jumped out of the bed and dashed out of the room, almost bumping onto his son. His wife followed at almost the same speed, forgetting to wear her night slippers as her cotton nightgown flapped behind her like the wings of a tropical butterfly.

Moments later, with tears flowing from their eyes, the family, standing on the stairs holding each other's hands, watched in silence as the African slave known as Melvin Davies, deeply engrossed in his activity; played one symphony after the other. The beautiful music hung in the air like a mist.

This truly was an amazing young man. No wonder their son was irresistibly drawn to him, Lloyd Davies thought as he witnessed this unbelievable sight. For what seemed like an eternity, they stood in silence as they listened to Sanza play the piano. That was when an idea struck Lloyd Davies. He looked at Sanza, who was still unaware of his audience, and looked at his son and wife. He smiled, and the smile turned to laughter of joy, which startled Sanza. He immediately stopped playing and stood up.

"Many apologies, master and madam. I did not mean to wake you up. I merely asked…"

"No, no, no Melvin," Lloyd Davies interjected with a wide grin. "How did you do that?"

Sanza cleared his throat and said,

"I don't know, master. I just heard young master playing and thought I could try."

This was incredible.

"Tell me something, Melvin. Do you think you can do that again?"

"Certainly, sir," Sanza said politely and immediately played Amadeus's first and second symphonies one more time. Lloyd Davies shook his head, again, in disbelief and amazement. This was beyond phenomenal.

It was then over the next three weeks that word was spread all over Raymond, Mississippi and nearby counties, informing wealthy plantation owners to meet at the Davies plantation at a specified date to witness an amazing spectacle. Lloyd Davies deliberately omitted to state exactly what this major spectacle was in an all-out attempt to fuel his prospective guests' curiosity.

Finally, the big day came. Luxury carriages were directed to the massive coach house located behind the mansion. This was after they were driven through a ¼ mile canopy of giant live oaks that formed an impressive avenue leading to the mansion. The mansion, itself, was a sight at this angle. Roman Doric plaster columns surrounded the house. The walls were 16 inches thick and built of solid masonry to give the look of an old fortress.

Over fifty guests were ushered into the gigantic dining room, where a 25-foot dining table ablaze with candles and rich, mouth-watering food awaited them. Five butlers and ten servants, all of them slaves, were assigned to tend to every need of the guests, many of whom were big name planters and intellectuals from all over Mississippi. It was for those reasons that all the slaves in the mansion were dressed in fine uniform, and cotton wigs, and white tights reserved strictly for occasions like this one.

The atmosphere was merry as the guests socialized with one another, all dressed in beautiful attire that was reserved only for the very wealthy. They talked in typical fashion of the rich in that era. Conversation rolled from one topic to the next with amazing ease. They talked about the previous year's crop production and the profits that came with it, the slaves they bought and sold, runaways, the price of cotton going up, and the impending war of independence in the North.

Many, particularly the men, were in favor of the war. It was about time they broke away from British rule. The empire was taxing them out of existence and being rich meant that they were the hardest hit.

"It is about time General Washington took a stand against a big bully like England," said Quincy Newton, a prosperous plantation owner from Biloxi.

"But from what I hear, that Washington fellow stands no chance at all. He is an inept general leading an undertrained and malnourished Continental army. The best thing for that man to do is surrender before he brings this country to ruins," said an oily-faced, fat man named Hubert Nance. He was a known cynic who was very wealthy, but always complained about everything that involved spending his money.

"But the British cannot figure out our militia, which happens to be the main key to total victory, and Washington has used it effectively," Quincy Newton countered. He was about to say more, but the soft ringing of a fork on a wine glass interrupted him.

This was a polite signal, telling the guests to come to order as the befitted host, Lloyd Davies, arrived at the dining room after all the guests felt comfortable with their surroundings and each other. He was with his wife, followed by Henry and Sanza, to whom nobody paid any close attention.

Sanza was dressed in white noble tights, knickerbockers, and a fitting jacket. His hair had been washed clean and combed with a nice part in the middle. His shoes were new, thus shining like mirrors although he walked quite awkwardly in them, similar to someone who was asked to walk barefooted on eggs without breaking them. In a rather rehearsed manner, Henry ushered him to the piano and stood beside him as if to reassure Sanza that his presence, alone, would shield him from the strange and piercing looks to which he was being subjected.

Looks said, "Who gives your black hide the right to sit among us when your place is really outside with the mules, donkeys, and pigs?" Some were beginning to wonder if Lloyd Davies, a respected and renowned planter, had lost his head.

"Ladies and gentlemen," Lloyd Davies said after helping himself to a huge piece of roasted lamb, soybeans, coleslaw, and mashed potatoes surrounded by a river of thick brown gravy, "I am honored by your visit. Now that you are here, it would not be fair of me to let you continue speculating about the purpose of this gathering. The story is both long and short, so I will be brief. Many years ago, I happened to be in Boston, not by accident, because I had prior knowledge that a ship full of high quality slaves from Africa was due. I got my share of slaves from the auction block. Among them was a young man I could estimate to be about sixteen or seventeen years old. That young man is the one seated at the piano." At that moment, Lloyd Davies smiled and pointed at Sanza Kazadi, the slave. "Ladies and gentlemen, allow me to introduce Melvin Davies."

The room was silent. The only sign that there were people there, other than their physical presence, was the irregular breathing. *What was Davies up to; all this for a nigger?* There were some whose faces turned red with fury as they now gulped down the wines at quick intervals. This did not deter Davies who simply smiled and nodded his head at the slave.

The nostalgic tune filled the room, immediately melting the tension. Stone cold faces started beaming—an effect only soothing music can bestow. No one in the room had heard anything so beautiful. It then occurred to the guests why they were there; Davies was showing off his slave, who could play the piano, to them.

After the tune, Sanza looked at his master, asking him with his eyes if he could continue. Lloyd Davies raised his hand, telling Sanza to wait a moment. There was a long silence before Davies spoke. Each person was still digesting the music they had just heard.

"Before you applaud," Lloyd Davies said, knowing very well that no one was prepared for that yet; he continued by saying, "may someone come forth and play a song no one has heard before?"

His audience could sense challenge in his tone, but still did not understand why. Finally, one of the guests, a beautiful young woman named Robina Smollet stood up. She had recently inherited her wealthy father's estate, making her the most sought after bachelorette. She had red hair and a captivating smile, marked by dimples on each cheek. She gracefully lifted her long dress a few inches from the floor and sat in front of the piano.

She played one of her compositions, which lasted close to seven minutes. The song was not a classic by any stretch of the imagination, but she did manage to get a standing ovation. After everyone settled down once more, Lloyd Davies nodded his approval and said:

"Now watch this, ladies and gentlemen. Melvin!"

"Yes, master," Sanza answered as he stood up from where he was seated—at the other end of the dining hall, away from the rest.

"Do your thing."

"Yes, master."

Sanza took his place in front of the piano, once again. There was an audible gasp of total surprise, shock, and amazement when Sanza played. The most surprised of all was Robina Smollet because it was her exact song that Sanza was playing. It was so exact that if one closed his eyes, he would swear that it was Robina playing her tune. There was a loud applause barely after he closed in on the last few notes.

"My goodness! How on earth did he do that?" exclaimed Baxter McDaniel, a reporter from the *Mississippi Sentinel*.

"That's just the question we keep asking ourselves," Lloyd Davies said. And at once, the room was buzzing with excitement.

"Let us see if he can play one of my old time favorites," one man said as he stood up to take over the piano.

"Most certainly," Davies had him ushered to the great piano, where the man played an old family song, which according to him, could be traced back to his pilgrim ancestry.

And once again, Sanza played back the song to the last bar. The author of the song, Robert Frances, was the first to applaud. Nobody in the room that day had witnessed such a sight, let alone could they imagine it. Sanza went on to play every person's request and favorite, which included, amongst many, Mozart's symphonies. The finale of the evening was when everyone was asked to open at random, a recently published 47 page pamphlet by Thomas Paine, *Issues Of Common Sense*, and Sanza would state word for word what was written on that particular page from memory.

Thereafter, it did not take long for Davies to become well-known among all the colonies that made up the Americas. He was known as the slave owner who possessed a slave called Melvin Davies, an African who possessed unheard of intellectual prowess. Lloyd Davies and Sanza were invited to perform everywhere. Invitations even came from as far as London, Rome, Vienna, and Paris, and that was how Lloyd Davies accumulated so much fame and fortune that exceeded his wildest dreams.

In no time, his son, Henry, enrolled at Harvard University at Cambridge, Massachusetts. Although he was a History major, he did, in his spare time, read countless journals and pamphlets of Law, Journalism, and Linguistics. By the time he was through with his schooling in 1792, Henry Thomas Davies was ready to take on a lifelong ambition, an expedition to the Dark Continent in search of a supernatural being who had started it all—Kahuru, the human leopard.

CHAPTER 20

THE IDEA OF LEADING AN EXPEDITION to Africa in search of the human leopard had not occurred by accident. This idea had started developing in his mind when Henry Thomas Davies was but a boy. As far as he was concerned, it was not a question as to whether such a being existed or not but where to find him. Given Sanza's chronicle, Kahuru originated from the Southern part of Africa. This part not very well-known to scholars and explorers of the day, except the southern tip of the continent known as the Cape of Good Hope, which subsequently served as a halfway station for ships en route to India.

With this concrete fact to build upon, Henry raided the family library and read everything there was that even remotely had to do with Africa. He interviewed world travelers and sailors who had dared the wrath of the seas and had kept notes. And over the years, he would ask Sanza to relate his experience with the human leopard over and over again, each time entering data that had been omitted in a previous conversation. This he did with so much zeal and meticulousness that it soon became a burning obsession.

Henry's big break came when his father sent him to Boston, Massachusetts to study at Harvard. Unlike Mississippi, this former colony had fewer farmers and more intellectuals. Thus, he was able to do much research over the next four years. He did not see much of Sanza nor his parents during this time as they were constantly traveling. His research ended when he graduated. By this time, he had accumulated volumes upon volumes of paper work.

He had spoken to University professors, clergymen, sailors, Paleontologists, Historians, slaves, former slaves, and every person who he thought might help his cause. He was caught up in an ecstasy of creative endeavor. It heightened his emotional awareness to the point where all of his existence was in those images of what lay ahead that flashed in his mind.

The final phase of his research was when he pitched his idea to two of Massachusetts's largest newspapers; *The Boston Herald* and *The Cambridge Journal*. It was not by sheer stroke of genius that he went to these papers. These newspapers had run an extensive article about a Southern slave owner and planter, Lloyd Davies, and his genius slave known as Melvin. The major difference that stood out from the rest of the papers that covered the same story was that they attributed Lloyd Davies' newfound fame and additional wealth to his slave. They even cared to publish an article about Sanza's story dating back to Africa, and of course, Sanza did not omit to mention his personal encounter with the human leopard.

On the strength of these articles, there were some slave owners who came forward with tales from some of their slaves who had either seen Kahuru or heard of him[§]. Henry took advantage of these leads and sought after those Africans. In essence, some of the testimonies, of the real witnesses that is, were not different from Sanza's. In some parts, there were astonishing similarities in detail.

So when Henry Thomas Davies pitched the idea that he was willing to lead an expedition in a quest to find the human leopard, he was met with little resistance. He wanted the full backing of the newspapers in terms of financing and arranging for a ship and crew. This expedition was also an all-out attempt to make a name for himself just as Sanza and his father had done. In February 1792, his request was formerly approved. He was to set sail from the Boston Harbor in the summer of the following year. In the meantime, a crew was being assembled, which included an experienced navigator and captain—an English man, Howard Lewis Scott, who knew the route to the coast at the Southern tip Africa very well. The crew

---

[§] It was always difficult to authenticate the so called eye witness accounts as many people had claimed to have seen Kahuru, when in fact they had just heard about him.

included master land-trekkers and some former slaves who still spoke numerous African dialects.

In preparation for this long and probably most dangerous mission, Henry decided to travel with some of the future crewmembers back to Raymond, Mississippi on land. The whole idea behind all this was to toughen himself and his crew for this forthcoming venture and to be hardened by the outdoors. Africa was alien to them. Who knew what dangers lay in store for them? There were tales of unspeakable horrors like primitive tribes that practiced cannibalism and sorcery amongst many others.

Needless to say, the journey to Mississippi was a long and hard one. It took three months of traveling in several carriages, and on the way, Henry and his party had to fight off a band of marauding Indians who tried to attack them. When they finally arrived at the plantation, the place looked like a shadow of its former self. Most of the slaves had been freed and had headed north. The few who remained had become sharecroppers. The mansion and the plantation in general had been put under the care of one of Lloyd Davies' trusted friends, a fellow plantation owner who lived two miles away. His name was Douglass Sullivan.

It was that very night, in the Height of the summer of 1792, when Henry sat in his room, which he had not seen for years, and gazed through the window across the courtyard towards the slave quarters. With tears in his eyes, he remembered the many nights he would sneak out, cuddle beside Sanza, and listen to tales about Africa and the triumphs of Kahuru. He wished Sanza could have been there with him to share that moment of triumph, a triumph that his lifelong quest was about to be fulfilled.

The last he had heard of Sanza and his parents was that they were traveling various parts of Europe. And while in London, Sanza had sent him a copy of *Gustavus Vassa: The African*. This was Olaudah Equiano's autobiography, published in 1789 and signed by the author, himself.

This was the story about a former slave who was snatched from Africa, and later on, this slave was among the many strong voices that helped abolish slavery and slave trading in the whole British Empire.

***

When Henry got back to Boston in early March 1793, he received an urgent message. It was from Leonard Pope, the owner of the *Boston Herald*. With a thumping heart filled with excitement, he quickly got dressed and rushed to the Pope residence on horseback. Since it was at the other side of town, he arrived there just before dusk.

Leonard Pope's mansion was located on one of the richest parts of Boston, where the houses were not cramped together creating almost nonnegotiable alleys that stank from standing water, garbage, and human secretions mixed with horse droppings. In this part of town, the houses were more stretched out. The streets were clean, and crime was almost non-existent. The streets were even free from packs of street urchins who were rampant on the east side. Even at this time of day, there was no smoke visible, as all houses had chimneys.

Upon entering the premises, a black steward (most blacks living in Boston were free) took care of his horse.

"Master Pope is waiting on you, sir," the man said as he led the horse to the back yard where the stables were located.

Henry took off his hat and walked along a beautiful winding path through a flower garden towards the entrance of the Pope mansion, a double-door fortress made of English Oak. He was about to pound at the door with his fist when the door opened ceremoniously, and behind it, stood a very pretty mulatto woman. She had wide eyes, high cheekbones, and thick, seductive lips that looked like they would drip honey. She was the housemaid and probably one of Leonard Pope's concubines, he thought.

The young lady smiled at him in a way that made Henry unconsciously raise his eyebrows.

"Mr. Davies?"

"Ah, yes," Henry said after an awkward pause.

"Mr. Pope is expecting you. May I have your cloak?" Her voice was angelic.

Keep calm Henry; you are about to embark on a lifelong quest. Stay focused, he thought to himself.

"Well, yes, ma'am," he managed to say and immediately bit his tongue. He had grown up in a society that never addressed a black woman as "Ma'am." They were even more inferior than the typical male nigger, but at the same time, these were beliefs Henry was trying very hard to discard. After all, his best friend was black, and he was warming himself to the idea that he was going to be seeing plenty of them in the not too distant future.

He took off his cloak and handed it to her, which she took and placed on a hanger beside the door, which was meant specifically for that purpose. She led him to the dining room. The candle chandeliers were already lit, and the house was warm. Leonard Pope was seated alone at the long banquet table. He immediately beamed when he saw the young man.

"Ahh! There you are, young Davies." Pope immediately stood up; he had been sipping from a glass of red wine and feasting on a plate of grilled T-bone steak, baked potatoes, casseroles, and thick gravy. Leonard Pope was short; he barely stood five feet six inches. At sixty-two, he still walked with a swagger that made his small, round belly bigger than it really was. They shook hands.

"Sit down, please. Can I offer you something to drink? Wine, brandy, lemonade?"

"Lemonade, please."

Pope rang a small bell that was beside some papers he was looking at, and almost instantaneously, the pretty mulatto woman appeared as if she was manifested by the shadows of the room.

"Yes, master," she said as she bowed cordially.

"A glass of lemonade for Mr. Davies, please, and bring it to my study room; that's where we will be, and we are not to be disturbed, understood?"

"Yes, master, anything else?"

"As a matter of fact, yes, Olga. Warm up a nice dish for Mr. Davies. I suppose he is very hungry."

It was as if he could read the other man's mind.

When in the study room, Leonard Pope poured himself a glass of brandy and gulped it down. He made a face, and a second helping also disappeared. He sat down at the other side of his huge desk and faced Henry. The walls of the room had large shelves fixed on them, each shelf filled with all kinds of books; it was obvious that Leonard Pope was an avid reader.

"Earl Buckner, of the *Cambridge Journal,* has backed off from his part of the deal of financing your forthcoming venture," Pope said as he smacked his lips shortly after Olga served the meal and left the study.

Henry Thomas Davies looked up in dismay. His mouth was half-filled with well-prepared fish and beans. He felt blood drain from his face. This could only mean one thing—the journey to Africa was not going to happen anytime soon, if ever; his lifelong ambition would be crushed; he would never get the chance to see the human leopard; history will never know him; he ...

At that moment, Leonard Pope waved his thick palm, indicating to the young man that he still had more to say.

"Fortunately, it has always been a habit of mine not to depend on other people's good intentions but on mine. That's why I am the proud and sole proprietor of one of Massachusetts's best newspapers. The expedition will go ahead as scheduled. You have my full backing. What I want from you is your guarantee that my paper, and only mine, shall own the exclusive rights to this story."

Henry had to refrain himself, which was no easy matter, from jumping up and giving the other man a bear-hug and a kiss.

"That goes without a saying, Mr. Pope, and if it pleases you, may I suggest that we keep the whole journey a secret in case reporters from other newspapers come snooping around?" He could hardly contain his exhilaration, and his voice gave it away.

"That is a good idea." He poured himself another glass of Brandy. This time, he merely took a sip. "I have a cellar in the basement in which I stored many barrels of these during the war," he diverted from the subject momentarily.

The war Leonard Pope was talking about was the American War of Independence, in which, General George Washington, who someone had called an inept general, had led his army to victory over the British after overcoming seemingly impossible odds. That same "inept general" ended up becoming the first president of the newly formed United States in 1789.

"One thing bothers me, though," Pope said, returning to the subject. "At our last meeting, you stated categorically that your plan on this mission is to seek and find the human leopard. My question to you, young Davies, is do you deep down in your heart believe that such a being does in fact exist?"

Henry, now a relieved man, managed a smile after attacking the fried fish on his plate with a fork and knife.

"You know, Mr. Pope ..."

"Call me Leonard, son. I know how formal you Southerners are," Leonard Pope interrupted.

"I used to ask myself that same question," Henry continued as if he did not hear what the other man had just said. "For years, as I grew older, I wanted to dismiss this story as another fairytale, but, Sanza would state facts about this being with astonishing detail that I, for one, was inclined to believe such a being did exist."

"Who?"

"Sanza ... I mean, Melvin Davies. Sanza is his real name," Henry answered.

"I see." Pope nodded thoughtfully. "And is it merely by his sole testimony that you decided to venture on this journey."

"Not entirely because when I came to Massachusetts, I was privileged to be in the company of some brilliant scholars who provided sound advice as to how to validate the authenticity of this being. Not many days would go by before I would ride on horseback and visit numerous plantations in as far off places as Carolina and interview many Africans fresh from the continent. Many had heard of Kahuru, and every single one of these Africans was unanimous about one thing—The human leopard originated from the very Southern part of the continent from a tribe that dwells at the foothills of magnificent mountains." He paused and drank some of his lemonade. Even though it was quite chilly outside, Leonard Pope's study had suddenly become uncomfortably hot.

"I have, over the years, written volumes about my encounters with Africans who had heard even a tiny bit about Kahuru and some of the things I tell you, Mr. Pope, will astound you. The human leopard does exist, and none of these Africans have seen or met Sanza Kazadi, excuse me, Melvin Davies, the original chronicler of this story whose mind I will never doubt." Henry was feeling more and more confident as he spoke. He did not care if the other man regarded him as a garrulous fanatic or simply out of his mind, but he stood firm in his belief that Kahuru did in fact exist, and he was going to find out one way or the other.

On the other hand, Leonard Pope started grinning. The grin turned into a laugh that violently shook his shoulders. Henry's face turned red with anger. He did not see the humor in anything he had just said. He was beginning to get the feeling that Leonard Pope was no longer enthusiastic about the expedition. After all, rich people have been known to flip for an idea and flip back on a whim.

"Mr. Pope, I would understand if you dismissed the whole thing as hogwash and not participate at all; after all, a number of people have told me to forget about the whole idea, that it is insane, and that I will be chasing a phantom or a figment of my imagination. I have chosen not to listen. I was hoping the backing of quite a pragmatic man like you will make this expedition a reality. But even if it means using my entire inheritance to make this expedition a reality, I will, but know this, without your help, it will take longer but still will happen."

He looked Leonard Pope straight in the eye. On the other hand, Pope liked what he saw. By laughing, he had Henry thinking that he had changed his mind. The truth of the matter was that all the lingering doubts he had about this expedition were quelled by this young man's conviction. He reminded him of George Washington in so many ways. When as a soldier under the then-general, he had been motivated, as were all others, to cross the Delaware at night and dare the English might. This sparked one of the great battles that was later to become a major turning point in their ultimate victory over the English and subsequently gave birth to a great nation.

"You misunderstood me entirely, young Davies," Pope said, the remnants of that laughter still playing on his face. "I am convinced, now more than ever, that you will succeed in your quest. And to show you how serious I am, I have these signed documents to prove." He handed Henry some thick legal pages.

The younger man could hardly believe his eyes. Right in front of him was signed legal documents declaring the expedition a reality. There was a special clause that stated that in the unfortunate event that the Kahuru story was nothing but a hoax, Henry was to return, and neither Leonard Pope nor the *Boston Herald* would require him to pay back any of the expenses incurred. Above all, no news about this venture would be leaked to any press if the journey proved to be futile. Henry's tongue was stuck to the roof of his mouth.

"I don't know what to say, Mr. Pope," he managed to say at last.

"One of those documents is yours to keep," he smiled reassuringly.

"Thank you very much, sir."

"It is my pleasure, young Davies." Then as an afterthought, he added, "You have four months before you set sail, so go and get you and your party ready."

"I will do just that, Mr. Pope."

He rode back to his house the next morning, feeling very upbeat. The quest to find the human leopard had begun.

<hr>

On June 11th, 1793, the ship, *Rock of Ages,* left the Boston harbor and set sail. She was a beauty at 125 feet long (over 30 meters), with an 81-foot foremast. It had twelve cabins in all, and each cabin had four berths. Among the sixty five men on board that day were captain Howard Lewis Scott, the master of the ocean, Benjamin Jamerson, the ex-slave who specialized in African Linguistics, eight trekkers, two officers, three cooks, and, of course, Henry Thomas Davies. The rest of the crew was to ensure Henry's safety while in the mainland. There was one person who should have been there that day, and that was none other than Sanza Kazadi, the man who made it happen. He was still in Europe with Henry's parents, and word was that he might have found a home there. It pained Henry that his friend had not been there to witness the end of what he had started.

Henry paced up and down the clean deck. There was nothing but the ocean ahead of them. He could feel the fresh breeze on his face. The sails billowed and strained against the masts and rigging ropes. The woodwork creaked gently whilst foam hissed under the lee rails, and the twilight sun sparkled on the sea. Henry closed his eyes and took a deep breath. The tang of salt pervaded everyone on the deck, and the air was clean and fresh.

"Africa, here I come. I come for you, and may the Almighty guide and protect us," Henry whispered to himself.

Meanwhile, in a cabin below, Captain Howard Lewis Scott had finished his routine inspection and ensured that they were heading in the right direction. He opened his log book and wrote this down:

June 11th, 1793 AD Rock of Ages set sail

Headed S.E.S. destination Cape of Good Hope

May the Lord be with us.

Henry remembered an ancient Chinese saying: *The journey of a thousand miles starts with one step.*

PART 4:
AFRICA

CHAPTER 21

"WHO ARE YOU PEOPLE?" Swathi demanded. His eyes were still focused on the white man. Henry looked at the interpreter and nodded. The interpreter was dressed in strange clothes similar to those worn by the white man. He cleared his throat before he spoke.

"Great king, my name is Mbulu, and the man here is Henry Thomas Davies. The other man with us is called Benjamin Jamerson; they came from a land far, far away across the great waters."

For the first time, Swathi shifted his focus and looked at the other man. He, too, was dressed like the white man, and although he was black like him, his feature seemed to point elsewhere. He definitely was not from one of the surrounding nations.

"What brings you here; better yet, tell me what tribe you are from, Mbulu, and how is it that you can understand their tongue?"

Only answers to these questions would help clear the confusion already mounting in Swathi's mind.

He wanted to know as much as he could about these strangers before he summoned his council.

"Great king," Mbulu answered, "My father is from the BaHurutshe clan. Many seasons ago, he traveled a great distance towards the great waters. No one knows why, but while there, he met my mother who is from the Khoikhoi people. My father became one of them. He settled and never went back to his people. Then one day, the white men, who had arrived in big canoes many seasons earlier, drove us out of our lands, and succeeded into turning some of us into servants who worked their farms—my parents included. I lived around these white people and soon learned their language. So, two moons ago, when these people came to shore seeking an interpreter, I became the natural choice since I was the only one they could find. I do not come from where they originate."

In essence, what Mbulu was saying was that Henry and his party had landed at the Cape of Good Hope, sought his services through the help of some English and Dutch farmers who had settled in that area, and continued with their journey, sailing around the Cape Peninsula until they reached Natal, dropped anchor, and began their trek into the interior in search of the Bakhudung village.

The great Bakhudung king nodded thoughtfully for a while, digesting the facts. He then turned and looked at Benjamin Jamerson once more.

"What about him?" The king wanted to know.

"He comes from across the great waters with the white man."

"Are you telling me that there are people who look like us in the lands far across the great waters?"

"Yes, great king."

"Then why doesn't he speak our tongue?" There was surprise on the king's face.

"According to stories that I have heard, great king, there are people who have been taken from their lands." Mbulu had to choose his words carefully here. "I mean, who left their lands in huge canoes and crossed the great waters in order to work on the lands of these white men."

Mbulu did not want to use the term "slavery" as this might put the white man's life and his party in grave danger.

"Now, what brings you here?"

This time, the question was directed mainly at Henry Davies. "Is it to take some of my people back with you?" Swathi knew why they were here but wanted, instead, to hear it from the white man's interpreter.

"No, no, great king," Mbulu answered quickly. "These men come on an entirely different issue altogether. They have heard about Kahuru, the human leopard."

There was a long and uncomfortable silence. So, it was true what his messenger had said. Swathi looked at the men seated before him. He thought he saw the white man's face twitch with excitement at the mention of the name, Kahuru. In Henry's mind, the tale that had started many years ago on a plantation in Raymond, Mississippi had just reverberated thousands and thousands of miles away. He was living the legend, seeing the people, and smelling the surroundings. Yes! It is safe now to say that the young Davies felt the spirit of Kahuru much closer than he ever had in his lifetime.

Suddenly, Swathi realized that this was a matter he could not handle by himself.

"Morongwa!" The king called, and almost as if from nowhere, the king's personal messenger appeared.

"Great king," the messenger bowed cordially.

"Summon the elders at once and do it quietly."

"As the king says, the great son of Muata, founder of our nation."

In a flash, Morongwa disappeared through the entrance. Swathi then turned to Mbulu and said,

"Our laws of hospitality dictate that you and your companions be well taken care of whilst under our protection. One of the servants will escort you to your various huts where you will be fed and bathed. I will send for you later after I meet with my council."

Mbulu translated. The two men nodded, and the white man said something.

"The white man says to thank you very much, O king," Mbulu said.

"Very well, anything else?"

"Yes, great king. There are other men we came with whom we left at the outskirts of the village."

"I shall send for them. Now go and rest, all of you."

The three men got up and bowed cordially to the king—a custom they had learned very quickly. Once outside, they were met by five royal servants who escorted them to their huts. The rest of the party joined them later. A skeleton crew, including the captain, had remained with the ship, which was still anchored at the coast barely 200 miles south. The arrival of these strangers did cause quite a stare among the villages, particularly the white man, who drew most of the attention. In essence this visit by Henry Thomas Davies and his party was epoch-making; dates of past and future events were to be described in relation to that visit.

Alone in his hut, Henry sat down and pondered his situation. The long quest was finally coming to an end. It took *Rock of Ages* eight months to reach the Cape, but before they could dock, they were hit by a terrible storm that subsided, thankfully, after one day. It had been a trying moment, and Henry had to thank his lucky stars that they were under the stern command of Captain Scott. He steered them out of danger, and they landed safely at the harbor of the Cape.

Later, Captain Scott stated that storms of that nature were symbolic of the Cape. He told the story of a Portuguese sailor, Bartholomew Diaz, who was sent to seek a sea route to India in the late 1400's. Diaz set sail around the African continent, and upon reaching the Southern tip, he was hit by several massive storms in succession and was forced to return home. Diaz later called that place the "Cape of Storms," but Prince Henry, the navigator, always the optimist, later renamed it the "Cape of Good Hope," after the good hope of one day realizing their dream of discovering the elusive route to India. A fellow Portuguese explorer, Vasco da Gama, discovered that route ten years later.

The journey from the Cape to Natal took two months with *Rock of Ages* dropping anchor on the morning of April 6th, 1794. They had dropped anchor two miles offshore, and the first boat to dispatch suffered a big mishap. Apparently, five crewmen on board overloaded the boat with equipment and food. Halfway towards the beach, the boat sank. Unfortunately, this was the section where the Atlantic and Indian Oceans meet, which creates a warm current all year long (known today as the Mozambique current) and a perfect place for the notorious Tiger sharks and the Great White Sharks. So it did not take long for several gray fins to break the surface and move in towards the helpless men.

Henry and the rest on deck could only watch in horror as the sharks devoured the five men. The next day, the remaining men exercised extreme caution, and the party reached the shores safely. That night, a vigil was held in memory of the five crewmen they had lost to the sharks. The following morning, Henry and his men began the long journey on foot towards the Bakhudung village.

They traveled all day and rested at night. The beauty of this unfamiliar territory was breathtaking, and Henry was compelled to enter everything he saw and heard into his personal diary. Benjamin Jamerson, on the other hand, would sit beside the fire long after everyone, except the two sentries, fell asleep and sketch beautiful drawings in his notepad. Besides being an expert in Linguistics, he was a great artist, too, a fine asset to possess if they were, in fact, to see the human leopard.

They arrived at the village after about 18 days of hard walking, sometimes getting lost and retracing their footsteps once more. What surprised Henry the most about his brief encounter with the Bakhudung, including their king, was that these people were not savage and warlike as he had been led to believe about Africans in general. On the contrary, the king displayed a warmth, wisdom, and courtesy that was hard to believe, the fact that he was seeing a white man for the first time not-withstanding.

Their village, even though primitive to the eyes of a westerner, was well-organized and clean. The villagers, themselves, were a bit timid at the sight of the strangers, which to some degree was understandable, but they were not the cannibals he was warned about on more than several occasions. And when the two young maidens came to his hut to announce that his food was ready, they did it with politeness that stunned the white man. Their timidity was not stemmed from inferiority but respect for another human being that seemed to have been groomed from birth.

Henry recorded all these observations in his diary, which had become a daily companion, and waited patiently for the king's summoning with a pounding heart. How he wished Sanza was there with him to share this moment.

——— ——— ———

Meanwhile, in King Swathi's royal hut, the council had just assembled. They all sat in a semi-circle arrangement and faced the king with the fire in between them. Noticeably absent from the council was the old man, Thulani, who had died two seasons earlier. The old Great had lived a full life, and being the Great that he was, he was given a state funeral.

It was a chilly morning, and all the elders had covered their shoulders with an extra skin blanket. The eldest man in the council, the wise man, Matiwane, coughed endlessly. They had all assembled moments after the king's messenger contacted them.

"Great council, I thank you for showing up despite my moment's notice. But you all know that a call of this nature advocates a matter that needs your audience and wisdom," the king announced and continued by saying, "A short while ago, I received a strange visit from three men and their party who come from far. One of them is a white man."

There was an audible gasp from the council.

"A white man?" Mophosho, the sub chief, asked in surprise. The *Batsamai* had spoken about the existence of such people.

"Yes, a white man. They seek to see and meet the human leopard."

This time, the gasp was long and hard; then, everybody started talking at once, and the king had to raise his hand to restore order.

"And just where exactly do these people come from, and how did they know about Kahuru?" Mophosho asked incredulously.

"Like I said, Mophosho, they say they come from the far lands across the great waters, the two men that is, the third, who happens to be their guide, comes the Khoikhoi clan. He also serves as their interpreter, for he can speak their language fluently," Swathi replied.

"Just how could they have heard of Kahuru if they come from the lands across the great waters?" This time it was Ndaba, the poet and orator, who asked.

"Word of mouth, Ndaba, is the only means I can think of. The great warrior has become a living legend. His deeds speak for themselves. We all remember many seasons ago when we were visited by two men from the Bamongo people who had traveled that great distance in search of

Kahuru in order to seek his hand in fighting off a mad gorilla."

Who would ever forget that day?

"True to word, great king," another man from the council said; his name was Lekwane. "We have, on our side, an immortal who has made our name resound even in far off lands," Lekwane boasted.

"Alright, what do these men seek of Kahuru, his help to quell some kind of evil?" Matiwane wanted to know amidst coughs.

"My understanding is that they just wish to see him in person—the white man in particular."

"How do we know that they come without evil intentions?" Ndaba, the Poet and orator, wanted to know. "You know evil comes in many forms, and one of its greatest disguises is the look of innocence on the surface." The poet drove the nail home with an intelligent choice of words, which as always impressed his audience.

It took a while for the king to come up with an answer, and when he did, he said,

"Great men, I understand your concern. I sincerely do. I am also aware that Kahuru is a state secret— his human identity that is. The only time we can call on him is when we are faced with a calamity we cannot handle, as was the case seasons ago when we were invaded by the giants and that wily imposter soon after. In short, great men, this matter is out of our hands; only the Oracle and sorcerer named Zebe can decide.

"Are you saying that these men should see the Oracle and request him to see Kahuru?" Mophosho asked in almost disbelief.

"Yes, Mophosho. That is all I can say at this moment."

"Having said that, will they be able to behold the Oracle, let alone go through the various stages?" asked another elder who had been quiet up until now. His name was Giyosi. He had fought bravely in the great wars against the outcasts and the Tompiki, such that upon retiring from active military duty, he was honored among the Bakhudung's elite—the Greats.

"They will have to undergo those if they really want to see the human leopard with their own eyes," Swathi answered.

For a while, there was complete silence; only the village could be heard. Lekwane was the first to break the silence.

"Perhaps we should try a divination before we reach a major decision."

The king smiled. What Lekwane suggested was a brilliant idea. Soon, a unanimous decision was reached, and Maru, the village doctor and diviner, was summoned shortly thereafter.

No one knew where Maru came from. True, he said he came from Bapong, but that was nowhere as far as the villagers were concerned. Some legend said he fell from the clouds, as his name suggested, and came to live among the Bakhudung many seasons ago. But by now, he had stayed so long in the village that people had ceased wondering from where he had come. To them, he was just a medicine man and a mediator between them and the spirit world.

Towards midday, the medicine man arrived at the royal hut. He greeted the men and occupied a stool situated at the other end of the room, where he could clearly see the king and his council. He was a well-built man with fierce and intimidating eyes. There was a baboon skull dangling from a string around his neck. This skull was obliterated by time. For a while, there was a disturbing silence.

Maru found his voice first,

"I am ready to start, great king."

Swathi nodded. He knew the witch doctor could not open his medicine bag in this type of situation before the king gave his consent to do so. For it would be an insult to his personal gods and such an insult that they would render his pronouncements ineffective.

"Let me have some dried pieces of meat and *itshwala*."

These were brought. Maru cut the meat into small pieces and threw them outside. He poured some *itshwala* as libation and muttered as each drop reached the ground.

"Ancestors of the night take this. Gods of the earth take this. Muata, founder of the Bakhudung, take this. And you, ancestors who help uphold the force of Good, take this."

He hung an amulet over the doorway to bar the way for evil spirits even though none would dare enter the royal compound; Maru's trade always demanded that caution be observed at all times. This was one of the traits that had made him one of the finest medicine men and diviners in the land. He then brought out his famous divination bones. Maru picked them up in both palms, blew at them, and tossed them to the floor. He repeated this exercise three times. After the third throw, he intently studied the bones. Afterwards, he slowly shifted his gaze from the bones to the king and his council, deliberately mounting the suspense in the room.

"You have called me about three strangers who came to see you this morning, great king," Maru finally announced to his stunned audience.

"That is true, Maru," Swathi confirmed, wondering at the same time what pronouncements the witch doctor had in store for them.

"Two of the strangers come from a land across the great waters, and they speak through an interpreter who understands their language. The main sight is the white man, hence this divination." It was a statement. His face was expressionless, but there was an incomprehensible look about his fierce eyes. Instead of looking outwards, they seemed to be staring inwards, into his head.

"That, too, is true, great witch doctor and diviner, he who sees what no mortal can see," The king concurred.

"It is about Kahuru, the human leopard. It is him they have come to see, right?"

This time, there was a unanimous "yes" from the whole council including Swathi. At that point, the king asked,

"How is it possible that they had traveled this great distance, overcoming numerous dangers; I would suppose, just to witness this immortal? Do they come with evil intentions?"

"That brings us to the second part of our divination, great king. Many seasons ago, when Kahuru was summoned by the Bamongo king to ward off that marauding gorilla, the human leopard stumbled upon some slave traders along the way. We all know the rest of the story. Among these freed slaves was a boy of about eight seasons; this boy was later sold off to the white men, who took him to their lands across the great waters. The boy was never heard of again. Nonetheless, he lived with these people, and prospered, and never ceased to relate the deeds and triumphs of Kahuru. What you witnessed today, great king, was the result of a tale the white man had heard many times before from this boy. It has been in the making for seasons. The white man's quest is to see the human leopard, with his own eyes that is. To him, unlike many others of his kind, Kahuru is not an enigma but a living, breathing, metaphysical being. And yes, these people come without evil intentions."

The king and his council listened to this weird and bizarre tale with their mouths agape. They had nothing to say as they stared at the witch doctor.

"Listen," Maru went on "who would dare to travel that long distance and, as the king put it, overcome numerous dangers if they did not have the strong conviction that the human leopard does, in fact, exist? I tell you, only the white man you met today, great king. It is not that he is out to prove to his people that the human leopard does exist; he seeks to satisfy a lifelong quest."

"What should be done then? We promised the oracle that we will never call upon Kahuru unless it is absolutely necessary," Swathi said.

"True to word, Swathi, but this is a matter in which the white man should see Zebe, himself, and make that request."

There was yet another audible gasp.

"So what you are saying is that the matter is beyond our hands?" Ndaba, the Poet and Orator, asked this time.

"Yes, all you can do is direct this man and his friends to the sacred mountains to face the Oracle. Teach them what to say and how to say it. In the event that they see Kahuru, they are to turn and go back and never set foot in this village ever again"

"But without us, they will be exposed to great danger if they are to face the Oracle," Giyosi said.

"Only if their intentions are evil. If they are, then their lives will be forfeited. No one ever trifles with the Oracle, but it must be made abundantly clear that they are not to come back to this village, but instead, to retrace their footsteps to the great canoe that awaits their return."

There was a long silence after Maru was through with his divination. It was the king who finally spoke,

"Maru, we thank you for your divinations. You may leave now, and you will be rewarded accordingly."

"It has been my pleasure, great king, and thank you very much. The gods and the great ancestors will see to it that you continue with your great reign that has made our name resound in far off places."

After the king left, Swathi and his council came closer and discussed, in low tones, their next plan of action.

CHAPTER 22

ONE MOON LATER.

THERE WAS NO MOON. A heavy wind blew that shook the trees made the shrubs sway sideways. The night thrilled as the ambivalent insect world came alive. The hooting of an owl, the distant roar of an irritated lion, and the chatter of night birds gave the night its ultimate terror. But, these sounds of the night were more or less part of the people's lives. In fact, a night without these sounds would be a scary one, but to Henry Thomas Davies, it was one vivid nightmare.

For the first time since he decided to take on this expedition, the young man felt fear in its naked and brutal self. Even the journey from Boston, Massachusetts to Raymond, Mississippi seemed like a walk in the fields, the several attacks from some Indian tribesmen notwithstanding. This was a different world, unknown to him, and bringing with it an unknown type of terror. He began to question the logic of having come to Africa in the first place as he walked awkwardly through the forest. On more than several occasions, he would stumble onto a thicket or a tree and negotiate his way back to the path, which looked like a dark tunnel. Curiosity mixed with courage matched his fear, hence he moved on.

Henry arrived at the mountains of the Oracle and sorcerer named Zebe just as the late moon streaked its weak rays through the clouds. The scene was ghastly. There were dark caves all around him, and on one occasion, he thought he saw some bats flying in and out of one of the caves. With a violently beating heart, he slowly felt his way through the rocks, thinking, as he climbed up the mountain, about if he would ever see home again. His scrotum shrunk as trickles of sweat ran down his armpits in rivulets. All was now quiet, except the beating of his heart.

Then all of a sudden, a voice from above tore into the silence like a knife.

"Who goes there?"

Henry Thomas Davies froze. For a moment, he thought he was either going to faint or die from fright. Instinctively, he looked up to where the voice came from. There was nobody as far as he could tell.

"Speak up, and speak up, now."

A terrifying echo followed the voice; Henry racked his brain to find his tongue.

"I am Henry Thomas Davies, son of Lloyd Davies. I come from a land across the great waters, known as the Americas." The Bakhudung had taught him well.

"What brings you here?" The terror that voice inflicted did not subside.

"With the great Oracle of Good willing, I have come to see the human leopard known as Kahuru."

There was a brief pause before the terrifying voice sounded again.

"Why?"

"From the time I was boy, I heard nothing but great deeds this warrior has achieved. It is not his power that I seek; all I seek is to see the immortal that has made me believe in the force of Good."

The Oracle was impressed with this answer.

"Well spoken stranger from far, but do you know that what you are doing could lead to your death in just a moment's notice?"

"Great Oracle, that is the basis of my true conviction. I am not afraid of dying in a quest I solely believe in, which is to see the immortal that conquers evil in the name of Good. Where I come from, I have seen evil in its naked form, and seeing the human leopard will save me from being sucked in by that evil known as slavery." Henry was now speaking like one possessed. The fear he had felt not too long ago had deserted him like an estranged lover; in its place was a bravado that even surprised him.

"Once again, you have spoken well and intelligently, young stranger from far."

Then at that moment, a crimson ball of fire flew from one of the caves overhead and landed a few inches from his feet. This time, Henry fell to his knees with fright. The ball of fire had come without notice. The Bakhudung and their King had not warned him about it during his gruesome one-moon training and initiation. The fire grew to a monstrous size; he looked up and for the first time, he saw the face of the dwarf Oracle.

"God Almighty!" He exclaimed, wide-eyed.

Then all of a sudden, the fire emitted thick fumes of smoke that caused him to gag and grab his throat as he coughed. His throat was burning as he gasped for air. Everything was spinning; he fell to the ground and rolled a few times, trying to fight the blackness that was quickly engulfing him, but he was powerless. He was spinning into an abyss, and that was his last conscious thought before he knew no more.

"Only the brave meet Kahuru," the Oracle said softly as everything turned back to normal.

The morning was bright, colorful, and lively. The birds sang their sweetest melody and monkeys and grey African parrots chattered; the evergreen forest was filled with exotic breeds of butterflies and insects. These were the sounds that woke Henry Thomas Davies with a start. He looked around and rubbed his eyes. He sat up and heard the gentle mummer of a nearby river. He slowly stood up, and exactly ten feet away sitting on a rock, staring at him with those fierce eyes, was Kahuru, the leopard man. He was still armed with the ultimate weapon—the spear of Good. Henry Thomas Davies screamed.

EPILOGUE

In December 1794, the ship, *Rock of Ages,* docked safely at the Boston Harbor, the same harbor made famous by the Boston Tea Party of 1773. The *Boston Herald* ran a full-length article on Henry Thomas Davies' expedition. Other newspapers across the country followed suit, making Henry one of the most sought after personalities for years to come. This included an invitation to the White House by President Thomas Jefferson and others. He did contact and meet Sanza; the latter had bought his freedom and remained in England a wealthy man. Sanza was later joined by Miss Robina Smollet, the same lady for whom he had replayed the tune at the Davies Plantation. It is believed that he later returned to his village in search of his family; that story has never been authenticated. Regardless, the final triumph of Kahuru in these people's lives was complete.

THE END

AKNOWLEDGEMENTS

SPECIAL THANKS GO TO: Faith Christa Ntuli, a woman blessed with multiple and incredible talents including being a great artist and friend who brought Kahuru to life. Carlos Ruiz, who gave me the book, *If You Can Talk You Can Write*, in essence telling me that there is no such thing as "writer's block". All my friends who helped expose my first novel, *Kahuru: The Making Of An African Legend,* to the world—especially Mbanefo 'MB' Akpong, Basima Dabutha, Tsogang Gaamangwe Sebina, Emmanuel Khumalo, Emmanuel Amissah, Gary Huer, Mario Conner, Pule Makgale, my wife and cherished companion Vivian Mafate, Vyerah Yende Mncube, Colin Porter, Moisiraele Prince Dibeela, my son, Uri Sebati Mafate, who as a toddler would come find me in the early hours of the morning, unaware that I was fully engrossed in writing this story —and many others (they know who they are). I will never be able to thank you enough.

AUTHOR'S NOTE.

'THE TRIUMPHS OF KAHURU' is entirely a work of fiction, and a product of my imagination. Any resemblance to actual persons living or dead is entirely coincidental and unintended. Save for certain historical places, names, and incidents, none of this story is based on fact. Research, hardly a priority, was not called upon, so mistakes made are mine and mine alone. Although, this novel is a follow up to *'Kahuru: The Making Of An African Legend'* published in 2001 by *iUniverse* Publications, the two books are not interdependent; they do however follow the saga of the human leopard.